Henrietta Chidlaw

Sunset and Evening Star

Henrietta Chidlaw

Sunset and Evening Star

ISBN/EAN: 9783337409234

Printed in Europe, USA, Canada, Australia, Japan

Cover: Foto ©Raphael Reischuk / pixelio.de

More available books at **www.hansebooks.com**

"Sunset and Evening Star."

In Memoriam

—of—

Rev. Benjamin Williams Chidlaw, D. D.

"At Evening Time it Shall be Light."

Zechariah xiv:7.

"*And I heard a voice from Heaven saying unto me: write, Blessed are the dead which die in the Lord from henceforth: Yea, saith the Spirit, that they may rest from their labours; and their works do follow them.*" Rev. 14-13.

UTICA, N. Y.:
PRESS OF T. J. GRIFFITHS.
1894.

Dedicatory Preface.

THERE are fathers and mothers, and the children of their children, scattered amid the woodlands and over the hill-slopes of the West, who were, by the blessing of God upon the early labors of my Sainted Husband, gathered into the Kingdom of God, and led to become Faithful Servants of the Lord. To these and to all who, like him, have the cause of Sabbath-school establishment and enlargement at heart.

THIS MEMORIAL VOLUME IS DEDICATED

by one who esteems it a comfort and a labor of love to send forth a second story of what he was, and what he did.

HENRIETTA CHIDLAW.

PREFACE.

———

IN THAT bright little volume entitled "The Story of My Life," Rev. Benjamin Williams Chidlaw, D. D., has himself supplied an account of some of the many interesting experiences of his eventful career.

To round out some of its aspects, and to complete the narrative of his life is the aim of this present memoir.

CONTENTS.

BENJAMIN WILLIAMS CHIDLAW.

CHAPTER I.

BIRTH, EDUCATION AND EARLY LABORS.

BENJAMIN W. CHIDLAW was born July 14, 1811, in the village of Bala, beside the lake Llyn Tegid, a "tarn" which travelers say is one of the most beautiful bits of water in the hilly country of North Wales. At the age of ten, he came to America, and, with his parents, settled in Ohio.

Rev. Dr. T. L. Cuyler, of Brooklyn, N. Y., once prepared as a sort of introduction to the "Story," a sketch of these early years, in which he says: "From his log cabin home he used to walk two miles through the forest to a log schoolhouse that had no glass in the windows—only oil paper.

" Our young hero bought a Webster's Spelling-Book with four pounds of butter, and some writing-paper by the sale of a few raccoon skins. The first sentence he ever read in Eng-

lish was that memorable first line in the spelling-
book, 'No man may put off the law of God.'
That is also the first sentence that I ever rub-
bed my boyish shins against, and I have always thanked Noah Webster for having started
thousands of American youth on the strong
meat of those terse and powerful words.
Young Chidlaw varied his studies of Webster
and the old 'Columbian Orator' with hunting
raccoons, fighting fever and ague, and helping
his poor widowed mother raise flax and weave
tow-cloth.   After completing his course in the
log school-house, he walked forty miles to
Granville, where he picked up some knowledge
of Latin from that grand old pioneer of Central
Ohio, the Rev. Jacob Little.

"This racy autobiography is tonic reading
for some of us old boys, as well as for the rising
generation.   In these days there are scores of
superbly endowed universities in our land, with
no end of splendid equipments.   College boys
now live on Brussels carpets, attend lectures in
brown-stone palaces, and spend more money in
boat clubs, and ball clubs, than linsey-woolsey
Chidlaw ever saw in all his days of hard fight
with poverty."

Dr. Chidlaw published in the Delaware, Ohio, *Gazette*, April 8, 1892, an article entitled, "My Mother's Spinning-Wheel," which is interesting as descriptive of this period of his life:

"In the garret of a spacious and beautiful farm-house in Radnor township, Delaware Co., Ohio, occupying the site of a log cabin built in 1809, this relic was found a few years ago. On it were these letters and figures, 'W. B., 1822, No. 146, for M. C.;' that is, William Boyd made it in 1822; the number manufactured was 146, and this one was made for Mary Chidlaw, my venerated mother. It is now held as a cherished heirloom—a specimen of early mechanical skill, and the manufacturing talent of the early pioneers. This old flax spinning wheel is a very suggestive reminder of my boyhood days spent in my log cabin home in Radnor.

"The log shop of William Boyd was two miles from my home, and always an object of great interest to the pioneer boy—the tools hanging on the log walls, and especially the lathe, attracted the eye and interest of the youthful observer, and when explained and used by the kind-hearted manufacturer, it be-

came a real pleasure, the memory of which
abides to this day.

"The clothing of the old Welsh settlers did
not last as long as the garments of the Israel-
ites did, so necessity taxed their skill and industry to supply their wardrobes.

"Flax culture was a necessity. A clearing
was made in the winter, and in the spring the
virgin soil received the flax-seed, which grew
luxuriantly, and was harvested and rotted by
spreading it on the ground to receive the autumnal rains and early frost. Then followed
the breaking, the scutching and hackling. The
tow was thus separated from the flax, and both
were in readiness for the spinning-wheel.

"The hum of the spinning-wheel and of the
reel, was the piano music of the pioneer home;
and, when echoed by the loom with its quick-
moving shuttle, furnished the tow cloth and
the fine linen so useful in those early times
when calico was worth a dollar a yard, and
money almost as scarce as hens' teeth.

"Then the Radnor boys figured in thin tow-
cloth pants and home-made linen shirts. Their
fathers, clad in the same apparel, laid broad
and deep the foundations of social, moral, in-

dustrial and religious life, that has kept the saloon out of Radnor, preserved its people from its demoralizing and impoverishing effects, and leaving for unborn generations the priceless inheritance of their good names, stalwart virtues, and sincere piety."

It will be remembered that Rev. Dr. B. W. Chidlaw had from early years been interested in the cause of Sunday-school instruction, and while discharging the duties of the ministerial office had extended his teachings to outlying districts, and organized many schools for the reverent study of God's Word.

In an address delivered years afterward in Baltimore, he said: " Sabbath-school work is in perfect harmony with the religion of Jesus Christ. This gives us confidence. Children, if brought up under the influence of the Bible, will be the life-blood of the Church as well as of the State. Many of the youth of our country are neglected or superficially educated. How can we reach them ? The American church has the power to gather them in and convert them. Let the retired list in the Sunday-school be broken up. The American Sunday School Union, national and entirely Christian in character, should go forth in its power."

The 28th annual report of "The Children's Home," Cincinnati, for the year 1892, says: "Early and constant friends have been passing away. One of these was the Rev. Dr. B. W. Chidlaw. He was the first editor of *The Children's Home Monthly Record*, and in the earliest days he assisted in placing the children in country homes. He frequently visited the children in the institution, and annually took them to visit him. The influence of his visits to them was that of a man of God; his voice, his pen and his purse were ever enlisted in our work."

CHAPTER II.

VOLUNTEER LABORS IN THE ARMY.

———

BY HIS labors as a chaplain and as a member of the U. S. Christian Commission, Dr. Chidlaw earned a full meed of praise and lasting gratitude at the hands of his countrymen; and approved himself in the sight of God and of men as a workman needing not to be ashamed.

He was the soul of patriotism. He loved his country almost as naturally as he loved his God; and the fact that it was his adopted country made no difference in either the degree or the quality of his affection.

It was most natural that such a man, who prized the land of his adoption with the utmost fervor, should spring forward with thousands as brave as himself, to defend the Union of these God-honored States when the dark crisis of the civil war was precipitated upon a distracted people.

"Inclination and duty," he records of himself, "led me to follow these brave patriots, who, to serve God and Country, hastened to the tented field, soon to realize the fearful realities of war."

We introduce here a part of an article published about this date in the *New York Times:*

"SUNDAY EVENING, AT CAMP HARRISON.

"The immense crowd of visitors had disappeared, mess was over, and twilight fell like a mantle on the camp. A group of soldiers were heard singing, and a multitude of attentive listeners was soon around them.

"Rev. Dr. Chidlaw having been invited to address the crowd, spoke of loyalty to God and to the Government. His impassioned and expressive words, showing that true faith made heroes in the Church and State, in ancient and modern times—that godliness inspired and nurtured true patriotism, and prepared the soldier for every post of duty and honor—secured the fixed attention of all his hearers."

The New York *Evangelist* prefaces a letter from Rev. Dr. Chidlaw:

"A week or two since we urged the great need of a supply of chaplains for the army, and those of the right kind. We are glad to see that this sort of men are already feeling an inward call to that work. It would be hard to pick out a better man for such a service than Brother Chidlaw, the veteran Sunday-school missionary.

"From the following letter just received from the West, it will be seen that he is already on duty at the camp near Cincinnati. A firmer friend and truer counselor could not be found for young men when they are in the camp, or when they march to the scene of war. May there be many of the like spirit and fidelity. We copy his brief letter:

"CAMP HARRISON, near Cincinnati, Ohio,

May 7, 1861.

"Ten days ago, encouraged by a deep conviction of duty, and a cordial welcome by the commanding officer, I entered upon missionary labors in behalf of the 3,500 true-hearted patriots here encamped. Greeting the men as a friend, I at once made friends, and secured their interest and confidence. Many knew me as the 'Sunday-school man,' who in former years spoke to them in their Sunday-school or at their 'big meetings,' and they were glad to see me, and promised to attend our religious services.

"Almost every evening, after mess, I hold a meeting. Singing brings my congregation together; then I occupy a half-hour in prayer and exhortation. I also visit the men in their quarters, talk and pray with them, and distribute tracts; and my calls are always well received. We have established a prayer meeting at 8 P. M. every night, which is sustained by the soldiers, and is exerting a blessed influence for good. These religious services make the soldiers acquainted with each other as brethren in the Lord. Thus their hearts are strengthened to serve God, and to aid each other in the Divine life. I hope soon to form a 'Christian brotherhood,' and to have our banner on the outer wall, witnessing for Jesus amid the trials and temptations of a military camp.

"I find abundant encouragement to labor. There is great need of religious effort. The camp is a wide and inviting field, yet there are difficulties which God alone can help us to overcome. Adult depravity is repellant; and tells me that there is more hope in the Sunday-school with children, than on the tented field with men never blessed with early religious training. The vast army now gathering to save our Government from overthrow, and the nation from anarchy, have strong claims upon the warmest sympathies of Christian patriotism. Let earnest prayer and faithful effort in their behalf every where abound."

"CAMP DENNISON, May 27th.

"At 3 P. M. Gen. Schligh's brigade mustered, (2,800 men) and formed in front of his quarters. The chaplain wished me to help him in the service. On the platform were some thirty officers, and before me, seated on the ground, this great congregation. I started with an expression which I heard from an old Revolutionary volunteer soldier, thirty-five years ago. He was with Washington at Valley Forge in that dreadful winter. He told me of sufferings that moved my young heart, and I asked him why they did not quit and go home? 'Well, my boy,' said the old soldier, 'we knew that God was with us and that He would see us through!' I spoke about ten or fifteen minutes, and I really felt that God was my present help.

"Later in the afternoon, I found in the quarters of the 'Oberlin Rifle,' a Bible class of forty members. Blessed sight! I was requested to address them. Then I visited two hospitals— not many sick.

"Thus passed another Sabbath, but I made no Sunday-school address. I am really hungry for the privilege of getting out into my special field again.

"I have rather a hard, uncomfortable life, but I feel like holding on, trusting in God, and rejoicing in my service for Christ's sake. Pray for me!"

And this devoted servant of God did "hold on." He made full proof of his ministry in hospitals, on tented field, and in the presence of popular assemblies, until at last on the collapse of the Confederacy—

"The war drums beat no longer
And the battle flags are furled."

CHAPTER III.

O NE of the regiments promptly responding to the call of patriotism was the 39th O. V. Infantry, of which regiment Dr. Chidlaw wrote "The 39th Ohio—a body of men fully equipped with arms, determination and courage."

He was asked to become its chaplain, as appears by the following telegram, bearing date:

"CAMP DENNISON, Aug. 14, 1861.

" REVEREND SIR:—At an election held this day by the field and company officers of the Groesbeck Regiment at Camp Dennison, you were elected chaplain to the regiment. Come up immediately or let us hear from you.

JOHN GROESBECK, (Colonel.) "

At first he declined the proffered honor, for reasons which seemed good to him at the time, but finally accepted the position.

The following letters and newspaper articles give an insight as to the occupation of Dr. Chidlaw during the interim of his election to, and his acceptance of, the chaplaincy:

" I am still doing what I can for the spiritual interest of our gathering hosts crowding the tented field. I did not accept of an appointment as chaplain—my duty to my dear wife and seven children stood in my way. I spend every spare day in the camp, and I bless God for the privilege. We are now gathering a better class of men. The religious element is strong, and if encouraged will be effective. Yesterday, as I read my text, I saw one company (United Presbyterians from Preble County, O.,) almost to a man, open their Bibles. This cheered my soul and helped me to preach. I found the officers unusually willing to help me. Thus I secured the arrangements I needed for our service, and at 10:30 full attendance. My heart is with the soldiers. I enjoy these labors, my poor soul feasts upon the gracious supplies the Master gives."

The Daily Times, Cincinnati, Aug. 5, 1861:

" On Sunday, at 10 A. M., the church call sounded. The men promptly fell into ranks and, in command of Major Noyes, marched to the grove, where a sermon was preached by Rev. B. W. Chidlaw. The good order on Sunday, and the interest manifested in the religious service, showed the high moral character of the soldiers, and that the officers are united and firm in maintaining the morals of the regiment."

In an address at the State S. S. Convention held at Binghamton in August, 1861, reported in the *Sunday-School Times,* Rev. Mr. Chidlaw thus relates a few striking incidents of his own experience in camp life, showing his manner of dealing with the men. He went among the soldiers at first a stranger. But soon a young man recognized him, " Ain't you the Sunday-school man?" " Yes," " I heard you sir, in our Sunday-school when I was a boy." " What company do you belong to ? "Company A, 7th Regiment." "Well, I would like to go and see how you live." " Very well. Here boys," turning to his comrades, "this is the Sunday-school preacher, he's going to our camp." And turning to him he asked, " Preacher, won't you mess with us ?"—and aside to his comrades, " Boys, mind, you musn't begin to eat until he asks a blessing."

Thus was the speaker recognized as a minister of Christ and as a Sunday-school man, a proud distinction—and thus he was enabled to get a hold upon the men, and to sow the seed of the Word.

The State of Missouri was then trembling in the balance between secession and loyalty. Before long the 39th Ohio received orders to that distracted section, and Rev. Mr. Chidlaw, (now formally commissioned as chaplain) accompanying it thither, was soon hard and successfully at work in the neighborhood of St. Louis. The following are extracts from published letters from himself and others:

"CAMP BENTON, Mo., Aug. 28, 1861.

"A line of well built barracks to accommodate eight or ten regiments will soon be finished and occupied. The parade grounds of the 39th, Col. Groesbeck, is universally admired, and for eight hours each day his gallant men are seen upon it. 'Getting ready' is the watchword of the officers and men.

"Every evening the chaplain, aided by officers and men, holds a short religious service, consisting of prayers, praise and exhortation. The voluntary attendance of so many, and their interest, indicate a high moral tone prevailing in the regiment.

"Col. Groesbeck has succeeded in removing

all the liquor-sellers and their stuff. When the regiment arrived these sharks were ready to devour and destroy. The colonel detailed Capt. Benjamin and a squad of his men to remove the nuisance, and complete success followed the march. The soil of Missouri was well moistened with bad whiskey and kindred fluids, and the owners put to an inglorious flight. The fathers and mothers, and wives and sisters of the noble soldiers, will thank the Colonel for this prompt and successful movement to crush the soldier's deadly foe.

"A striking feature of garrison life, in the shape of a somewhat unusual religious ceremony introduced into the regimental routine of the 39th Ohio through the influence of the bold chaplain, is here noted.

"At dress parade, every evening, at the request of the officers, they have worship, consisting of reading the Scriptures and prayers. The service seems to impress favorably the regiment and the crowd of visitors in attendance from the city of St. Louis. On Sabbath morning the regiment is marched out to an adjoining grove, where divine service is held. The

B

attendance of the soldiers is good, and some individuals seem deeply impressed.

"One man in particular called for a personal interview. His attention had been arrested by a thought uttered by the chaplain, that a soldier must be loyal to his God as well as to his country. He felt that he had been a rebel against God all his life, and desired to know what he must do to be saved."

"CAMP BENTON, Sept. 1, 1861,

"THIRTY-NINTH REGIMENT, O. V., U. S. A.

"At 10:30 A. M., this regiment attended divine service in a beautiful grove kindly thrown open by Colonel O'Fallon. The chaplain, Rev. B. W. Chidlaw, preached a sermon from Mark 12, 17, ('Render to Cæsar the things that are Cæsar's, and to God the things that are God's'). During the service the men appeared greatly interested. At 2 P. M. a Sabbath school was formed—the chaplain was chosen superintendent, and ninety-five of the soldiers were enrolled as scholars. An hour was profitably spent in the study of the fifth chapter of Matthew. A religious association called the 'Christian Brotherhood of the Thirty-ninth Regiment' is formed, and a large number of the men have enrolled their names."

The special reason for uniting in the bonds of a "Christian Brotherhood" is thus explained in the *American Messenger:*

"In some of the regiments of our army, the plan of establishing church organizations has been attempted, but found impracticable, on account of the various sects and creeds. Rev. Mr. Chidlaw, the chaplain of the Thirty-ninth Ohio, has adopted a plan that has been followed by others, for bringing together the Christian soldiers to help each other, and combine their influence for good upon others in a Christian assoc'ation or brotherhood, to continue during the war, leaving their church relations undisturbed."

(TO A CHRISTIAN BROTHER.)

"CAMP BENTON, Mo., Sept. 3, 1861.

"When we used to meet as soldiers of the Cross on the battle-fields of Zion, in the Miami Valley, little did I think that, as chaplain of the 39th Ohio Regiment, I should sit in my tent and address you a letter. How mysterious the ways of God! How wonderful that we should be called to vindicate the authority, and to maintain the supremacy of our government against a gigantic and wicked rebellion. I feel its dreadful reality on this tented field—the bristling of ten thousand bayonets, and the tread of a thousand horses training for the clash of arms and horrid strife.

"For the sake of preaching Jesus to the 1,000 gallant men composing this regiment, I accepted the appointment, and am now in active duty as chaplain. Our officers show that they appreciate the value of religion, and of religious efforts among the men; and in this important regard I am highly favored, and feel much encouragment. I find a goodly number of pious men, avowed friends of Christ, in all the companies of this regiment.

"B. W. Chidlaw."

"Camp Benton, Mo., Sept. 16, 1861.

"My experience in the work shows that the soldier's Sunday-school is an arm of Christian service on which we may safely rely. The Sunday-school army on the tented field may fall into line and hold its regular drills—the heavenly tactics may be studied, and 'onward we move,' emblazoned upon its waving banners.

"At 2 P. M., I was invited to aid Rev. S. R. Adams, chaplain of the Twenty-sixth Indiana, encamped near us, to form a Sunday-school.

"We planted our banners beneath the outstretching branches of a majestic oak, and soon 150 soldiers, with their Testaments, gathered around. The enrollment was very promptly despatched, as an old veteran it was my privilege to give the general orders.

"My address drew up a large crowd, and we were compelled to spend the time in addresses. I was followed by the chaplain and gallant colonel, who, with several of his staff, have enlisted as teachers; and from the Christian character and Sunday-school labors of Col. Wheatley, of the Presbyterian church at Indianapolis, I have no doubt but that he will be in the Sunday-school what he is at the head of his noble regiment—the right man in the right place.

"Our Christian labors in the camp must be prompt, discreet, and advanced movements; early, earnest and prudent labors on our part are indispensable to success."

"BENTON BARRACKS, Mo., Sept. 17, 1861.

"I have met over thirty regiments since last June, and I am confident that the religious and moral element in each is such as to secure the establishment and maintenance of a vigorous and useful Sabbath-school.

"I find a field of labor among our sick. The soldier, in the time of affliction, needs all our offices of humanity and Christian sympathy, and I find him very susceptible to religious influence. If I can do him good when sick, he is very likely to regard my efforts to minister to his spiritual wants when he is in health. Thus I am enabled to win the confidence of the men, and they recognize me as their friend. Friends in Cincinnati gave me paper and envelopes; by supplying the men, I can induce them to employ their leisure time in writing—quite an improvement on idle conversation, loafing and card playing. My little library of twenty-five volumes is doing a good work. 'What is this among so many?' is my trouble. Blessed with health, and pleasure in my humble services, let me ask my friends to remember the chaplain and his pastorate in their prayers, and to do all they can to lead our gallant soldiers to Jesus, salvation and heaven.

"B. W. CHIDLAW."

"BENTON BARRACKS, Mo., Sept. 18, 1861.

"This vast encampment, four miles from St. Louis, with its substantial and commodious quarters, is a place of great military activity. Regiments are going out, and others filling their places almost daily. The cavalry and artillery force is very large, and increasing.

*   *   *   *   *

"Last Sunday, Gen. Curtis commanding the Post, issued an order for divine service in the great Amphitheatre on the Fair Grounds. A very large crowd assembled, and Rev. B. W. Chidlaw, Chaplain of the 39th Ohio Regiment, preached. His voice, manner and subject held his immense audience in fixed attention to the close."

So striking and memorable were these Fair Grounds services that we are led to insert this extended report of the Fast Day observances ordered by President Lincoln in 1861, which is taken from the St. Louis *Daily Democrat* of September 27th.

"The Rev. B. W. Chidlaw delivered a sermon yesterday afternoon in the Amphitheatre, to an assemblage of troops, the novelty of the occasion having drawn there also many citizens,

who, as well as the soldiers, were highly delighted.   To those who have been in the Amphitheatre when it was crowded with gaily
dressed citizens in time of peace, witnessing the
exhibitions of fast trotting, &c., the scene of
yesterday was a striking contrast.   Thousands
of belted men lifting their voices in sacred song,
and listening with grave faces and uncovered
heads to the words of religion, formed an impressive scene, not soon to be erased from the
memory.   The preacher spoke from a temporary pulpit placed in the arena between the
benches and the green sward that surrounded
the pagoda, and his words were plainly audible
to every one of his immense and attentive
audience.

"The services commenced with the singing
of that old and beautiful hymn:

> 'All hail the power of Jesus' name,
>   Let angels prostrate fall.'

"During the singing, the First Regiment of
the Douglas Brigade, a neatly uniformed and
splendid body of men, preceded by a fine band,
ascended into the Amphitheatre, and secured
seats in military order.

"After prayer by one of the chaplains who

were seated by the pulpit, the hymn beginning,

'O Lord of hosts, Almighty King,'

was sung by the entire congregation, in a very impressive manner, to the tune of Old Hundred.

"The reverend gentleman took his text from the Second Book of Chronicles, seventh chapter and fourteenth verse:

'If my people, which are called by my name, shall humble themselves and pray, and seek my face, and turn from their wicked ways; then will I hear from heaven, and will forgive their sins, and heal their land.'

"The sermon was delivered in a very impressive manner, and was received with profound attention by the vast audience." [The sermon will be found in the Appendix.]

It was with reference to this stirring pulpit experience on "Fast Day," that Rev. Mr. Chidlaw afterwards wrote:

"Regiment after regiment marched in, and I found a precious opportunity to address an immense congregation. In the centre of this vast assembly my heart was overwhelmed with the responsibility of my position. The General and his staff, and quite a number of our field

officers were among my most attentive hearers.
Such examples of interest in Sabbath observance and divine worship, on the part of our
officers, will greatly influence our soldiers, and
aid our chaplains in their duties." And again:

"In my discourse I endeavored to show the
conditions of Divine deliverance in times of
national calamities. I have now found that
congregations of soldiers can, by proper authority, be gathered for the stated worship of
God, and that this service is not a weariness,
but a delight to our gallant men.

"Preaching to the brigade makes me known
to the men, and scores of them, as I pass
through the camp, greet me as friends, and
many of them as brethren beloved in the
Lord."

The spirit of the true soldier shows itself in
the following:

"BENTON BARRACKS, Mo., Sept. 23, 1861.

"With Company K, and forty men from the
hospitals, I am still separated from our regiment. This separation is to all of us very un-
pleasant and undesirable. We want to be with
our gallant comrades, and to share their toils
and dangers.   *   *   *   In a few days

we shall have a commodious hospital opened in camp, and the necessity of transporting our sick to the city in ambulances will end. I always found our men in the hospitals very cheerful, and many of them reading their Testaments and Hymn-books. And when I handed them letters from their friends, as one man said, 'it did them a world of good.'

"In the evening, at the invitation of Capt. D. G. Robb, of the Indiana Flying Artillery, under marching orders, I preached to his command. A few candles stuck to the trees illumined our sanctuary. My hearers were seated on the green sod, and with profound attention heard my message. To-day, this fine company expect to leave for active service. They are in very good spirits, and when the time comes for action, the country will hear from Capt. Robb and his gallant command.

"Since Saturday, three regiments from Illinois have arrived at the Barracks, and one left. Three sister States, Ohio, Illinois and Indiana, are pushing a strong and glorious column into Missouri. Our Commander-in-Chief, General Fremont, the illustrious Pathfinder, hails this outpouring of troops with pleasure, and we are all inspired with confidence."

Dr. Chidlaw's hopeful optimism finds illustration in the language of a letter home, bearing date Sept. 27, 1861:

"Our forces are concentrating, and in good spirits. In the name of the Lord, we shall meet the foe, crush his power and give peace to this distracted, bleeding portion of our beloved country. The broad dimensions of the rebellion, and the importance of adequate force to suppress it, now loom up before our people, and will secure corresponding action. This assault upon our national life, this malignant and powerful effort to destroy our union, and subvert our government, must be met, and I bless God that we are meeting it. If our friends in Ohio, Indiana, and Illinois could see the spirit and working of secession as it is seen in Missouri; if they could hear the weeping, lamentation and woe of its victims, no longer would they feel indifferent, or stand aloof from this glorious struggle to save our country from anarchy and ruin."

With the inspiration of the impressive "Fast-day Service" previously referred to, still upon

him, Chaplain Chidlaw wrote to Hamilton Presbytery, which met at Cleves, O., Sept. 27th:

"I feel that I am at the post of duty, as the
pastor of one thousand men, and I find encouragement to do the work of the ministry among
them. I preach twice every Sabbath, superin-
tend my Sabbath-school and hold a prayer meeting. I am here encouraged by our officers, and
find favor in sight of the men."

Under date of Sept. 30, 1861, he writes to
the *Cincinnati Gazette* from " Benton Barracks,
Mo:"

" At 10 A. M. I preached to a large congregation made up of parts of three regiments. My
Bible class was well attended, and the soldiers
manifested quite an interest in the study of
God's word; and many of them by their replies
to my questions exhibited a thorough knowledge
of its divine teachings. At 4 P. M. I preached
to Captain Constable's command at the arsenal.
The officers and men, as we worshipped God
beneath the forest trees, encouraged my heart
by their fixed attention and evident interest in
the services. I am always favored with the
hearing ear of our soldiers. I need no guard to
keep them around me, and I never discharge

my ministerial duties with greater pleasure. For which I would humbly thank my Divine Master and the co-operation of my officers.

"P. S. I have just received a letter from Col. Groesbeck, mailed at Brookfield, Mo., Sept. 28th."

The good colonel cheers his chaplain, separated from the regiment, by writing, "You know that we should all be happy to have you with us, but as we are so divided, I shall not order you here. Stay where you think you will be most useful."

CHAPTER IV

CONTINUED LABORS AS A CHAPLAIN.

———

FROM the beginning of his army career, Dr. Chidlaw mingled well advised efforts for the material comfort of the soldiers with the spiritual attentions of the ministerial office, laboring to provide "things necessary, as well for the body as the soul."

Doing the one, he did not leave the other undone. Therefore it was said of him with truth: "The soldiers bless him wherever he goes,"

In the Cincinnati *Times-Star* of Jan. 6, '62, appeared a reminiscent article signed "The Old Chaplain," (a title which our hero, it seems, was fond of calling himself) describing the operation of "Getting Overcoats for the Boys in '61."

"In July, 1861, the Thirty-ninth Ohio Volunteer Regiment was organized at Camp Dennison. Its staff officers consisted of Col. John Groesbeck, Lieut. Col. Gilbert, Maj. E. F. Noyes, Surgeon O. W. Nixon and Chaplain

Chidlaw. The rank and file numbered 960 enlisted men well officered. Early in August,
1861, the regiment, armed and equipped, was
ordered to Missouri. *   *   * The regiment on landing at St. Louis was ordered to
encamp at O'Fallon's grove, a few miles north
of the city. Here we spent a month with several Iowa, Illinois and Ohio regiments. Early
in October the Thirty-ninth was divided into
two battalions and ordered for duty on the
lines of the Hannibal & St. Jo and the Pacific
Railroads, then infested with bridge burners
and bushwhackers,—the terror of all loyal citizens and the destroyers of their property.
Guarding the bridges and relieving the country
of bands of secession desperadoes required much
exposure, and, for the want of overcoats, our
brave boys were suffering from the chilling
winds and autumnal rains.

"About the middle of October the chaplain
was informed that Col. Groesbeck wished him
to go to Columbus and see Gov. Dennison in regard to a supply of overcoats for his suffering
soldiers.

"At once he departed and the next day met
the Governor in Columbus and delivered his

message. The kind-hearted and patriotic Governor gave earnest heed to the statements and pleadings of the chaplain for his suffering parishioners while heroically saving the State of Missouri from seceding and entering the Confederacy. The Governor said that if he could find the overcoats he would give an order at once, but he knew of none that could be secured. Then he consulted with Capt. Wright, the quartermaster, who was also deeply interested and anxious to aid the Chaplain in his mission.

"The Governor gave me a letter to the U. S. Q. M. in Cincinnati, urging him to furnish the overcoats and forward them at once to Missouri.

"The U. S. Q. M., Capt. Dickerson, was found at the Burnet House. His response to the appeal of the Chaplain and the Governor of Ohio was rather laconic: 'If I could furnish overcoats I would send them to West Virginia.'

"Greatly discouraged and perplexed, as the Chaplain passed the corner of Walnut and Fifth streets, he saw soldiers' overcoats in front of the store of Cole & Hopkins. He knew Mr. L. C. Hopkins, and told him his mission and made in-

c

quiries about the overcoats. Mr. Hopkins replied that they had a contract to supply the State of Illinois with 10,000 overcoats, to be delivered at Springfield, Ill., but that he did not think they could furnish the goods for several weeks if the State would order them.

"Inquiring of his bookkeeper, he found that they had a thousand overcoats at Springfield in excess of their contract. The Chaplain with a sample coat and the price, took the first train for Columbus, and in double quick time made his way to the Governor's chamber in the State House.

"Calling in some of the Staff, the coat was carefully examined, and finding the price satisfactory, Gov. Dennison gave the Chaplain a letter to Gen. O. M. Mitchell, commanding the post. This brave soldier and true patriot expressed his great pleasure that the coats could be purchased and at once issued the order.

"This important document was delivered to Messrs. Cole & Hopkins and the order to deliver the goods at Springfield to the representative of the Thirty-ninth O. V. I.

"On the street the Chaplain met his Quartermaster Edwards, who was sent on the same er-

rand by Lieut. Col. Gilbert, of the Second Battalion, encamped at Syracuse, Mo., who was delighted that the goods had been secured. On
the sidewalk the Chaplain gave the order to the
quartermaster, who the same day left for Springfield, and the Chaplain, to spend a day with his
wife and children at their pleasant home near
Cleves, O.

" In a few days the overcoats were issued to
the boys amid shouts that made the welkin ring,
and rousing cheers for Gov. Dennison and Gen.
Mitchell."

The three letters following indicate the sense
of satisfaction the good Chaplain had in his work,
and the earnestness of his desires for the improvement of the tone of army life:

"OCT. 22, 1861.

" The religious services in our regiment and
the general conduct of our men is producing a
very happy influence on the people around us.
They begin to learn the true mission of the Federal army—that we are sent not to destroy but
to preserve and to heal this bleeding land.

" I find many ways to do good to our men,
and to win their confidence. Far from home,

and experiencing some of the realities of soldier life, I find my cup of mercy overflowing.

" My labors are congenial and pleasant, and I trust not altogether unprofitable. All I need is a large portion of the Master's spirit, and a renewed baptism of the Holy One. Brethren pray for me and for all the Chaplains in the army, and the thousands of precious souls under our pastoral care."

"October 23, 1861.

" Here amid the desolateness of a wicked rebellion, far from home, and experiencing some of the realities of a soldier's life, I feel thankful for the work God has given me to do, and the pleasure I find in endeavoring to do the work of the ministry among these brave men imperiling their lives to sustain the Government and preserve the Union. There are many and serious difficulties in the way, and discouragements that almost crush the heart, but God is with us, and we must not mind these ' lions in the way.' Earnest and prudent efforts for the intellectual, moral and spiritual improvement of our soldiers, the distribution of good reading, personal, friendly conversation, and public services on the Sabbath, are appreciated and acceptable to the great mass of men, and as chaplain, constrained by the love of Christ and philanthropy, we may find a wide and hopeful field. 'Pray for us.'"

"October 24, 1861.

"Secession and desolation have gone hand in hand over this beautiful, but now wretched country. A year ago this town had 4,000 inhabitants; now, nearly half the houses are deserted. There are six meeting-houses, four of which are closed.

*   *   *   *   *

"Last Sabbath our Colonel led his men to divine service. They appeared neat and cleanly. Their arms gleamed in the sunbeams. The Baptist meeting - house, the largest in the place, and which had been closed for months, was opened for our use. The men stacked their arms in front, leaving guards to watch them, and the house was filled with an attentive audience.

"I preached from the text, 1 Cor. xvi. 13: 'Quit you like men, be strong'—showing the Scripture idea of true manhood and its achievements.

*   *   *   *   *

"At 6 P. M., we held our prayer-meeting in the Baptist church. Some three hundred were present, and we had a good time.

"My congregation dispersed very quietly and orderly. By and by, as we were marching along, the voice of singing fell on my ear, proceeding from the front of our line. Scores of my soldier parishioners, many of them brethren beloved in the Lord, united in the song:

> 'We're traveling home to heaven above,
>   Will you go?
> To sing the Saviour's dying love,
>   Will you go?

"The effect of this solemn and spontaneous praise was impressive and inspiring. Gushing out of the hearts and lips of these noble men, it thrilled every portal of my heart and soul with rapture. We find that religion pays in camp just as well as at our distant homes and sanctuaries. God helping us, we intend to keep the banner of the Cross flying over our tented field, to follow on to know the Lord, and to do all we can to have all our comrades prove loyal to God and his law, as they are to their country and its constitution.

" Brethren, pray for us, and fight valiantly for Jesus on your spiritual battle-fields at home."

The worth of the energetic Chaplain was quickly recognized and generously appreciated, as appears in a letter dated

"CAMP PRENTISS, CHILLICOTHE, MO.,
Oct. 30, 1861.

"We have been over to visit our neighbors, the 39th Ohio. The 39th is considered here a well-officered regiment, having two leading spirits that do great honor to their rank and position. We mean Col. Groesbeck and Rev. B. W. Chidlaw, the Chaplain, whose energetic mind and industrious habits render him very popular and useful with his regiment in numerous ways outside of his post.

"C. C. SPRAGUE."

The liveliness of Chaplain Chidlaw's sense of humor and the vivacity of his style may be gathered from the following letter, dated

"CAMP PRENTISS, MO., NOV. 1, 1861.

" One morning this week a private in Co. I, Captain Benjamin, reported that he had found an enemy secreted in a ravine near our camp. The captain, having some experience in the

service, with his first lieutenant, accompanied the man to the bush, in which the enemy, armed to the teeth, lay concealed. The foe was found in the thicket, carefully covered with brush and weeds. Advancing cautiously, the covering was removed, and a veritable 'red head'—forty-one gallons, Cincinnati brand, came to light. The enemy thus captured—this masked battery —was in position for his deadly work, but had not belched out a single charge. The captain pronounced his doom, and the lieutenant, armed with a 5 lb. axe, inflicted the righteous sentence, and out rushed the evil spirit. * * *
A liquor dealer, whose ungodly traffic our excellent Colonel had suppressed, had located the 41 gallon masked battery in the bush, with the intention of drawing out in 'smalls' to sell. This fellow, in the wreck of his 'red-head,' will learn that the 39th O. V. is death on Secesh, and its potent ally, bad whiskey.

CHAPTER V.

CAMP life at Macon, Mo., is graphically portrayed in a series of letters of different dates in November, 1861.

"November 13.

"Three months of ministerial labor on the tented field has identified me with my parishioners and my pastoral duties. The people of my care are a heterogeneous mass, made up of river men, laborers, farmers, mechanics, and I regret to add, not a few who had no occupation—drift-wood on the stream of time.

"Unimproved intellects, and hearts unblessed with moral culture, no taste for reading or improvement, and the great temptations in camp life to idleness and vice, are features in my field of labor that frequently chill the heart with despondency. Our arms hang down in feebleness, and our strength fails.

"But here lies the field, with all that is precious in the undying interests of a thousand

men; here, victories involving eternal weal are
to be gained or lost.   Our weapons are not car-
nal, and greater is He that is for us than all that
are against us.   Therefore, in the name of the
Lord we have set up our banners."

"November 25.

"In this camp we have at present some
twenty Secession prisoners taken by Colonel
Foster of the Twenty-third Missouri, in his late
expedition.   They were entertained in an old,
dilapidated frame house, and well guarded.   One
was Gen. H—— (so called by his comrades, and
famous as a drill-master in the service of Gen.
Price).   He sported a dingy-looking blanket
with much gracefulness, and evidently ranked
high in the esteem of his friends around him.
Another had on his uniform, gray-colored and
thread-bare, in which he fought the 'Lincoln-
ites' on the battle-fields of Missouri.   We entered upon a free conversation on various top-
ics.   Soon the subject of Secession was introduced, and one of them asked me to give them
my view upon it, adding, 'We don't hear much
on your side of the question.'

"Standing in the midst of an audience of
rebel prisoners, on the floor of the guard-house,

to speak of law and government, treason and rebellion, was an unexpected opportunity of serving my country. They heard me with respectful attention, and invited me to visit them again.

" Most of these men were armed with rifles, shot-guns and a home-made sabre. I was told that the manufacturer (the owner of a country blacksmith shop) in the service of rebeldom, for four months had been hard at work on this weapon, and that he had supplied the army of C. S. A., Jeff. Davis, President, with no inconsiderable amount of this sabre, something like a small scythe, in a zinc scabbard."

" November 27.

"On Sabbath, I called on a party of Confederate prisoners, taken captive by a Federal exploring party in Missouri, and addressed them. They wished me to do so, and heard me with respectful attention as I spoke of loyalty to God, and to the government which He had ordained, and which they were charged with attempting to destroy, and held for trial. Three-fourths of these men knew but very little of the great issues at stake, or what they were really doing. Led by demagogues, they rushed

into the madness of treason.   I inquired if they
had schools, and if the churches were opened
in their neighborhoods.   They gave me no reply except, 'I don't know of any.'   This is
the dark feature of Secession.   It has infatu-
ated the people, kindled the unhallowed fires of
discord, strife and bitter animosities, ignored
religion, which teaches loyalty to God and to
Cæsar, and closed its sanctuaries.   Long ago
its leader and its convention voted the 'school
fund' to aid rebellion.   Hence the school-house
is closed, and the youth, neglected and ungov-
erned, are following in the wake of their mis-
guided parents.

" The cold weather and the want of water-
proof tents have subjected us to many serious
discomforts.   If we quarter here for the winter, I hope to have a large room where we can
hold public worship, and have our camp library,
and newspapers, and desks, for letter-writing,
and 'cheer' for the gallant soldiers, that will
cultivate their hearts and improve their minds.
With the help of officers, I hope to have classes
in various branches of science, and to establish
a lyceum.   We must do something of this kind
to save our men from the effects of mental in-

activity, and from the tides of demoralization that are sweeping over our tented fields."

" November 27,

"To-morrow is Thanksgiving in our loved Ohio, and the 39th will observe it in Missouri. We shall have preaching at 11 A. M., and also an evening service. In visiting the hospital this morning, after giving all the comfort I could to the twenty patients, most of them convalescent, I passed through the kitchen and beheld the kind-hearted steward and his faithful helpers hard at work on " fat shanghais and two fine turkeys," preparing them for Thanksgiving dinner for the brave boys of the hospital. By the looks of a pail filled with eggs, a pan of rich milk, and delicious-looking pumpkins, they intended to give the real finish of a 'Down-East' Thanksgiving feast.

" Honor to the hearts and hands that work for the sick soldier, that fill his heart with joy, and his tin plate with the nice, the good and the substantial."

The discourse of Chaplain Chidlaw on this Thanksgiving day was afterward printed in pamphlet form, as indicated by an appreciative newspaper notice:

"A Thanksgiving Sermon, preached before the Thirty-ninth O. V., U. S. A., at Camp Todd, Macon, Missouri, November 28, 1861, and a Sketch of the Regiment. By Rev. B. W. Chidlaw, Chaplain. 12mo., pp. 24. Cincinnati: George Crosby.

"A discourse admirably adapted to its occasion and audience, redolent of cheerful piety and pure patriotism. Mr. Chidlaw is one of the religious institutions of the West, and his many thousand friends will be gratified to read his views of army life and duties, here so clearly and characteristically set forth. The Appendix to the pamphlet gives a history, list of officers, and necrology of the Thirty-ninth, which have obviously been prepared with much care."

The great catastrophe of the Civil War had inevitably interrupted many former lines of life, and introduced multitudes to new and strange occupations. Sensible of this Chaplain Chidlaw, in 1861, wrote to his good friend, Geo. H. Stuart, Esq., of Philadelphia;—

"Camp Thirty-ninth, Ohio Vols.,
Macon, Mo., 1861.

"G. H. Stuart, Sup't, Ref'd Pres. Ch. S. S., Broad St., Phila. :

"How strange, that the old Sunday-school

missionary should sit in his quarters in a U. S. military encampment, midway between the Missouri and Mississippi and, while the cold wind is howling around him, address a letter to his young friends in your Sabbath school. A thousand men called him to be their pastor, four months ago in their own loved Ohio, and God helped him to respond. In this regiment one-half of the men never attended Divine worship before they came to camp. They were river men, and had no Sabbath—farmers and laborers, never went to the sanctuary; one-fourth attended divine service occasionally, but had no ties binding them to the house of the Lord and His worship. The other fourth attended and were interested in sanctuary privileges, and the half of this fourth are professors of faith, and most of them witness a good profession: that is, out of 1,000 men I have 125 who are avowedly true disciples of Jesus Christ. Now, why is it that so many are careless, hardened and indifferent to the claims of personal religion? I have found the answer—these men never attended divine worship at home, never went to Sabbath schools; no parental and pastoral labor won their young hearts to the Bible, the Sanctuary and the Saviour.

And now, as their Chaplain, my heart is crushed by their irreligion and wicked lives. They came to hear me preach. Their ignorance of divine truth, and their wicked hearts are so repellent that it seems impossible to interest them.

If God crowns our armies with success and our government is saved from the traitors that would destroy it, I hope to assume my humble work among the children of the West, with all my heart. Oh! If some one had gathered these 500 or 700 thoughtless, hardened men into the Sabbath school, and if they had been taught of the Lord, how different would be the spiritual and moral aspect of this encampment, and how blessed my labors as their pastor. My soldier Sabbath school is sustained, and I hope profitably. I have some two hundred names who attend, but not all at once. Most of our men attend my morning service in the open air. Now we are without a place of worship. Our sanctuary on the broad bosom of the prairie, beneath the blue canopy of heaven, cannot be occupied this inclement weather. A small Presbyterian

meeting house which we found vacant (for secession soon closes the church and the school-
house) is occupied by us, but it will not accommodate one-fourth of our men. Our prayer-
meetings are held here. There is encamped
near us the Twenty-second Mo. Volunteers, Col.
Foster. They have no Chaplain, no books, no
tracts. My stock is exhausted and they are left
famishing for the bread of life; but I look for a
supply from friends in New York in a few days.
As far as I could learn, the religious and moral
element in the regiment is very feeble. I found
a few Christian brethren who had their banner
on the outer wall. At their invitation I went
over one day last week, to make an address on
Temperance. These good men, vexed with the
filthy conversation of the wicked, rallied around
me. I took my position on a wood pile near the
centre of the camp, and we engaged in singing.
This brought my hearers together, a congregation of 150; about the half of them had dingy
pipes in their mouths; and I felt a chill come
over my heart as I saw their listlessness and indifference. On my left was a party playing
cards, gambling with camp currency, (sutler's
tickets). I tried to pray, but the heavens were

D

as brass; indeed, I felt so disheartened that I thought I would retreat; but I dare not do this. I soon saw two men deeply interested, and this broke the ice, God gave me freedom and my hearers became more attentive, but the gambling went steadily on.   After talking on intemperance, the use of tobacco and liquor, I turned my battery on card-playing and gambling.   I gave them, for I had a clean sweep, a few shells; at first they looked up to see where the trouble came from, and soon they gave up the ground, and I felt that victory had perched on my banner, for which at the close we thanked God, and went our way rejoicing in God our strength and shield.

" My dear youth, make the most of your present religious privileges; early give your hearts to Christ, bear the yoke in your youth, and follow on to know the Lord. In your labors of love, remember the neglected children of the great West. Help the American Sunday-school Union. to gather them into the Sunday-school fold, and to Jesus, the good Shepherd.   God bless your Sunday Schools.   Pray for me, your friend.

"B. W. CHIDLAW."

Mr. Chidlaw quickly found in pursuing his pastoral labors in camp, that a good supply of reading matter was essential to the best results, intellectual and spiritual,—hence the circular of an Eastern publisher which is printed here, followed by the appeal to which it refers:—

" Sabbath School Depository, }
9 Cornhill, Boston, December, 1861. }

" My Dear Sir:

" If any apology is needed for troubling you with this Circular it must be found in the urgency of the case to which I invite your attention. The following letter was penned by one whose name is a household word in the homes of nearly every family in the free States of our beloved country.

" For a quarter of a century, Rev. Mr. Chidlaw has labored with a zeal that knows no abatement as a Sunday-school missionary in the West. At the call of his country he has left his Sabbath-school work, home and family, to share the fortunes and privations of the camp. As chaplain of the 39th Ohio Volunteers, now in Missouri, he sends to his Eastern brethren the following urgent appeal. It breathes all through the earnest spirit of the man, and will, I am sure, touch a sympathetic cord in the hearts of all who read it. I promptly sent him a small lot, but ' What are these amongst so many?

"Will your school lend a helping hand? If the amount be but small, it will swell the aggregate. 'Many a little makes a mickle.' I wish to send this dear brother a large box of books right away. Will you help me to do so? Direct to No. 9 Cornhill, Boston.

> "Sincerely and truly yours,
>
> "HENRY HOYT."

(Camp of Ohio Volunteers.)

"MACON, Mo., November 20, 1861.

"DEAR BROTHER HOYT:

" After reading (with tearful eyes) the 'Drummer Boy,' which you sent me, I loaned it to our drummer boys, and they were much interested in reading it. Now the book is going the rounds of our tents. I have just heard from it. A man has just called on me at my quarters, to get his book exchanged, and told me, I got hold yesterday of that 'Drummer Boy,' and I sat down on the hay in my tent, and read it through; and more than once it started tears. This morning while it rained, I read it aloud to my mess-mates, some of them were moved to tears. Then I let it go to be read in another tent.

"Dear Brother Hoyt, do get help from my

friends in Boston, and send me ten or twenty of the 'Drummer Boy,' and a lot of other kindred books, published by yourself and others. As winter is closing on us, I find that a library circulating among the thousand men and boys in my parish is what I need. Don't lose time; send 50 or 100 of Brother Stone's sermon— its living fire warms our patriotism. My copy, sent by you is on the rounds. One of our officers was taking fire from it when I saw it last.

"God bless Brother Stone for throwing up such a breastwork around the old doctrine of Paul and the Puritans—yea, of God Himself. Dear Brother, excuse my entreaties for aid. You know the friends in the Sabbath schools who will help you fill a box with good books.

" P. S. We closed all the rum shops around us yesterday.

"Your brother,

"B. W. Chidlaw.

(To the *Congregationalist*, Feb. 4, 1862.)

"Through the liberality of Eastern friends I have introduced into my regiment a library of 300 volumes. To-day, as I visited the sergeant's quarters, where they are kept, I found that nearly all were out. And in passing through

our barracks I saw them in the hands of the
men.   I gave to the Third Missouri Cavalry,
Col Glover, 400 'Cromwell's Bible,' 200 'Something for the Knapsack,' and about 50 volumes
of excellent books."

(To the *Cincinnati Gazette*, Dec. 4, 1861.)

"On last Saturday I supplied 250 copies of
' Something for the Knapsack,' in Col. Bishop's
Black Hawk Cavalry Regiment, encamped near
us.   The colonel thanked me for my labor of
love in behalf of his men, and invited me to
preach for him on the Sabbath. About 1 P. M. I
reported myself to the colonel as ready for duty.
I found two large log heaps blazing finely, and
quite a crowd around them.   The day was
quite cool, but calm, and these rousing fires
kept my congregation comfortable; and I delivered my message on the text, ' Be thou valiant for me, and fight the Lord's battles,' to a
very orderly and attentive audience."

"PALMYRA, Mo., Dec. 22, 1861.

" Orders to march reached us at Macon on the
4th inst.   That day and night, via the railroad,
brought us to St. Joseph, and on the 5th, General Prentiss, at the head of 2,000 men, left for
the countries on the north side of the river,

where disloyalty abounded. The moral effect of our march was excellent. The people were led by their leaders to expect an army of 'Jay-hawkers,' 'Hessians,' 'Nigger Thieves,' and 'Barbarians' to devastate the country.

"General Prentiss, an able soldier, a good man and strictly temperate, led his gallant force through the country in perfect order; no acts of lawlessness were committed, nor deeds of violence. This secured the respect of Seces-sionists, and inspired the confidence of every loyal man in the power and purpose of the Gov-ernment to maintain the Constitution and laws. Thousands, we trust, were led to see the folly of rebellion, and to understand the general ob-ject of the U. S. army, and will henceforth re-turn to allegiance and duty.

"With the work of a Chaplain in the camp, six months of service had made me quite fa-miliar; but what can he do on the march, is a question to be answered by experience.

"Our force was made up of Ohio, Illinois and Missouri men, strangers to each other; and the excitement, toil and trials of active service in the field, placed many 'lions' in the way of the Chaplain.

"One evening, our tents pitched, our supper
of hard bread, mess pork and coffee enjoyed,
musing over the camp fire, I heard the voice of
praise falling on my ear from a distant part of
the encampment.

"With a Christian brother I walked in the
direction of the singing, and we soon found ourselves with a few brethren beloved in the Lord.
The night was mild, and a full-orbed moon
turned darkness into day. I was invited to
preach. Several men went around and announced divine worship; and, as we sung another hymn, a large congregation assembled.
Standing in a wagon, I spoke the words of eternal life, and my soldier-hearers appeared deeply interested. At the close, many gave me
their hands and bid me God speed in my labors
as Chaplain.

"One morning, having missed my breakfast,
I was accosted by an officer, who invited me to
preach that night in his regiment. I told him
that depended upon whether I could get anything to eat; that our stores were exhausted,
and the prospect of supply was very gloomy.
' Oh, sir, I have plenty; walk with me;' and by
his camp fire I was regaled with 'slap-jacks,'

fried bacon and cold water; and my soul was refreshed in conversing with a Christian brother. His parents in North Carolina had been members of the Presbyterian church under the care of Rev. Dr. C——. At home, in Iowa, he served the Lord, and was a ruling elder in the church of Christ; and in the army his faithfulness failed not.

"I saw a squad of soldiers entering the yard of a farm-house on the road-side. I followed them and heard them ask the farmer in the most respectful manner for a few apples, saying they had no money to pay for them. The man was sullen, and refused, saying he had none. One of the men said to me, 'Chaplain, look into that out-house, and see what a pile of apples this mean 'Secesh' has.' The men would have helped themselves, but I told them that would be contrary to our orders; that soon they would find the right kind of a man, who would give them plenty of apples. They quietly left the yard, and I told the man that his inhumanity and lying deserved a different treatment; but ours was a mission to maintain the law; hence, he and his property were safe. Gen.

Prentiss told the truth, 'that his men could be trusted anywhere.' "

One of the stories told at the Y. M. C. A. meeting, evidently was that which has been preserved in a newspaper account under the title of

"AN ARMY INCIDENT."

An incident of one of the marches of his regiment in Missouri, was narrated by Rev. Mr. Chidlaw as follows:

"One venerable old lady, her wrinkled face radiant with smiles, her tremulous voice burdened with blessing upon the soldiers bearing the stars and stripes, came to the road to greet us.

"Several of our men said to me, 'Chaplain go and shake hands with the good old mother for us all!' I did so, and my hand never received a more cordial shake. 'God bless you, and every soldier in your ranks!' gushed from her patriotic heart, bedewed with her tears. The loud shouts of our gallant soldiers told the response of a thousand hearts. Still holding my hand, she said, 'My father was seven years in the Revolutionary war. I have lived for seventy-five years in this land of law and order, protected and blessed. There is my home. Last week the Secessionists entered it—took my bedding, my provision and my horse. Thank God, I have guardians to-day in the Union army, and I expect to see my country delivered from all its enemies, and to feel safe at my own fireside."

Continuing my conversation, I found that my patriotic old friend was a mother in Israel, ripening amid these sore trials for a better life. ' Ah, my friend, this secession has well nigh driven religion out of the country. Talk to me of Jesus and his redeeming love ! Fifty years ago I found my Saviour; for Him I live, and in Him I hope to die,' were the touching words of the aged pilgrim, loyal to her God and her country."

Another incident, of a nature both grotesque and pathetic, is described in the records of the period :

" Last week a drunken soldier (not of the 39th) by his gyrations and boisterous behavior disturbing the public peace, was made to pay a novel penalty for his indulgence. An empty whiskey barrel was brought into requisition, one end being knocked out and a large hole sawed in the other.   The young Bacchanalian, with his head peering out of the barrel resting on his shoulders and reaching below his knees, marched along the streets, labeled 'a drunken soldier.'

"In due time the mortified youth was released from his oak-whiskey-saturated covering, and we hope will hereafter have nothing to do with intoxicating drink.

"By and by the drunkard-maker was found, and subjected to the same punishment.   He was labeled—'shame on the man who sells liquor to the soldier.'   While this fellow was parading the streets with his new overcoat, the negroes were much delighted, and when he was released, they gave him a grand 'Good-bye, old fellow, guess you no sell whiskey for some time after dis!'

"They had a reason for this gratification, for not a few of them had suffered on his account."

This deserved tribute to the regiment with which the Chaplain was always proud to be connected, appeared in the Palmyra *Courier*, in February, 1862, a paper whose staunch loyalist sentiments found expression in the stanza of a

song, then popular, appearing conspicuously in
its columns, underneath a cut of the flag:

'The union of lakes—the union of lands—
The union of States none can sever—
The union of hearts—the union of hands—
And the Flag of our Union forever.'

" The five companies of the 39th Ohio, station-
ed in Palmyra since the middle of December
last, left here on last Wednesday morning,
under orders for Benton Barracks, St. Louis.
We note the departure of this corps of noble
soldiers with feelings of sincere regret. Not
that their absence leaves the loyal population of
Palmyra and vicinity exposed to the attacks of
a malignant and revengeful enemy (for the ever
faithful, brave, and vigilant Third Missouri
Cavalry still remain here) but because we miss
the pleasant daily intercourse with its truly refined and gentlemanly officers and privates,
which it has been our privilege to enjoy during
the season of their residence here. And this
feeling we find is participated in by all the people
of Palmyra. The uniformly kind and affable
demeanor of the officers, in their daily exchange
of sentiments with our citizens, won for them
the good opinion of all, and long will the period

of their sojourning in Palmyra be remembered with unalloyed satisfaction.

"As a body, this regiment compares most favorably with any in the service. Its excellent discipline, prompt obedience to orders, and above all, the high moral tone pervading the masses of the privates, render the regiment in the highest degree efficient and reliable.

"For the moral tone of the rank and file not a little credit is due to their excellent and indefatigable Chaplain, Rev. B. W. Chidlaw, than whom there is certainly not a fitter Chaplain in the service. Ever ready to minister to the wants of all the men, and to assist and console them in all their trials and difficulties, and eminently popular in his daily intercourse with the regiment (as with all Union men outside of it), he has attached the entire body to him by ties of the warmest affection. He is doing a noble work, making the 39th Ohio a regiment of model men and, as a consequence, model soldiers."

With which testimonial of regard belongs this reciprocal expression of Mr. Chidlaw's:

"On leaving Palmyra, where we have been quartered for nearly two months, in behalf of the Thirty-ninth Ohio Volunteers, U. S. A., I would express our obligations to our numerous friends for uniform kindness, and deeds of benevolence, that have added so much pleasure to our sojourning among them. To Uncle Sam's Daughters, whose labors of love, and welcome visits have cheered and comforted our sick, and encouraged those who ministered to their necessities, we return our heartfelt gratitude. Those 'Daughters' are known by their work of love, and their names and philanthropy will ever be cherished. While on the field, and when at our firesides at home, these devoted ladies, friends of the soldier in his sorrow and sadness, will be fondly remembered.

" To the Presbyterian Church, in whose neat and commodious Sanctuary the 39th held its Sabbath and week evening religious services, we tender our grateful thanks. Long will we remember the genial hospitality and pleasant society of our numerous friends in Palmyra.

"B. W. CHIDLAW, Chaplain.

"Feb. 11, 1862."

CHAPTER VI.

"OUR HOSPITAL CHAPEL."

———

IN 1864, a little paper-covered pamphlet, from the pen of Rev. Dr. Chidlaw, was issued, entitled "Our Hospital Chapel,"

"In the spring of 1861, this location, sixteen miles from Cincinnati, on the Little Miami Railroad, was selected by Gen. McClellan for a camp of instruction. Thousands of brave men, responding promptly and earnestly to the call of their country, were here mustered into service, armed and equipped, and soon ordered into Western Virginia and Missouri.

*   *   *   *

"In the spring of 1862, the beautiful plain on the west side of the railroad, skirted with wood-covered hills, became the site of a long line of neat and commodious hospital barracks, with comfortable accommodations for over two thousand patients. After the battles of Fort Donelson and Shiloh, a large number of sick and wounded soldiers were brought to Camp Dennison Hospital, and much public interest was manifested in the relief of their sufferings, and in efforts to supply their spiritual wants. These ministrations, so kindly bestowed by the friends of the suffering soldier, were always welcomed and appreciated by the officers and the patients. The hand that ministered in clean clothes and nutritious food, the heart that throbbed with Christian sympathy, and the lips that opened to speak of Christ and salvation, found among these brave sufferers a wide and inviting field.

" With many others it was the pleasure and privilege of the writer frequently to engage in these delightful labors, distributing little delicacies, always thankfully received by the grateful recipients, to give religious and miscellaneous reading to the men who were "hungry for something to read," to speak words of consolation and hope to the distressed and sorrowing, and, as opportunity allowed, to hold divine service when hundreds of deeply interested men would gladly and devoutly hear the words of eternal life. Until the summer of 1863, these public religious services were held in the open air, or in some unoccupied ward or mess-room.

E

"The necessity of a chapel suited to our
wants, and centrally located, was seriously felt.
Several efforts were made to secure its erection
by the Government or private benefactions, but
without success. On a bright morning in June,
while visiting the different wards, the men with
genial smiles of welcome cheering my heart, a
lovely youth,—still a sufferer from his wounds,
—inquired, 'Shall we have meeting this morning?' Others united in the request, and through
the kindness of Dr. W———, one of his wards
was opened for 'meeting,' and soon filled with
a crowd of attentive blue-coat hearers. Most of
my congregation were standing, and among
them I observed four wounded men supported
by their crutches, listening with fixed attention
and evident interest to our Gospel message.

"Such men, with a desire to attend divine
service, certainly deserved a sanctuary and a
seat, where, with their fellow sufferers, they
might worship God and enjoy Christian fellowship. Constrained by the necessity of the case,
and trusting in God and the friends of the soldier, I called upon Col. Neff, commanding the
post, to inquire what could be done in regard
to the erection of a hospital chapel. The Col-

onel, ready for every good work and word in behalf of the soldier, at once and with great cordiality favored the enterprise, informing me that the Government gave him no authority to erect such a building, and that we must depend upon the liberality of friends to provide the means. We knew that our children loved the soldiers, and that their young hearts and willing hands could be interested in this work of love. The Sabbath school scholars of England built a missionary ship that carried the Gospel around the globe; our own Sabbath school children did the same; and we resolved to try and build a hospital chapel with the aid of the Sabbath school scholars of Cincinnati.

"On the following Sabbath I secured pledges of aid from eleven of our schools. The next day our plans were laid before Major-General Burnside. This brave soldier and true man gave the enterprise his unqualified approbation, adding: 'By all means, a chapel must be built; I will inquire if the Government can build it; if not, please call on me for twenty-five dollars, to help the Sabbath-school scholars in their kindness to the suffering soldiers.'

"The next day General Burnside issued an

order to have a chapel erected, giving our children the opportunity to furnish it. The officers
in charge located the chapel on a beautiful spot
near the centre of the line of barracks, render-
ing it very convenient and of easy access.

"Seats for five hundred men, and a valuable
melodeon, were provided by the children of a
few Sabbath schools. Other friends in Cincinnati donated the pulpit, the carpet, the window-
shades, the lamps, the chairs, the bell, the Bible,
and five hundred hymn books.

"On the 14th of August, this neat and commodious chapel was dedicated with appropriate
religious exercises to the service of God. The
occasion to the soldiers and their friends was
replete with delight and pleasure. We felt that
God accepted the offering, that His blessing and
approbation would rest upon the good work thus
auspiciously begun.

"Soon after the opening of the 'Soldiers'
Bethel,' I spent a delightful Sabbath at Camp
Dennison. In the early morning I visited several of the wards, conversing and praying with
some of the sufferers, who were drawing near
to life's last hours. Some of them were deeply
impressed with the solemnity of their condition,

and anxious to make sure work for eternity; others, alas! were careless and unconcerned.

" In a cavalry regiment encamped east of the railroad, we found a good congregation, and preached to them Christ and the Resurrection.

" In the afternoon we held funeral services in the chapel. A loyal Virginian, a brave and faithful soldier, was to be buried. His remains were carried from the ' dead-house ' by his comrades to the chapel which was crowded with an attentive and solemn congregation of convalescents, paying their last respects to the memory of a fellow soldier. After appropriate services, a long procession, with muffled drum and solemn step, moved to the ' soldiers grave-yard,' and laid in the silent chamber of death another noble soldier to sleep, with nearly four hundred of his comrades, till the day of immortal awakening, when they that ' sleep in Jesus will God bring with Him ' to be forever with the Lord, to rest and reign, in the glory which is to be revealed.

" Our prayer-meeting at the hour of the setting sun was largely attended. Our blue-coat brethren ' fighting for the flag, and living by the cross,' offered devout prayers—made earnest exhortations, or told us what the Lord had done for their souls.

"In this social worship, where our brethren were bold for Christ, and faithful in duty, we enjoyed precious tokens of the Divine presence, sweet Christian fellowship, and a good preparation to preach to a crowded audience at a later hour. The theme of our discourse was "The service of Christ," in its nature and rewards, with an earnest appeal to every slave of sin, by virtue of the emancipation act proclaimed by a dying Saviour on the Cross, to strike for freedom and to become the servants of God. The cloud of mercy which overshadowed us at the Mercy seat lingered over the assembly as we preached the word of life. At the close, I invited all who were serving God, who loved the Saviour and rested on Him for salvation, to stand up. At once, nearly one hundred of our soldier brethren stood up for Jesus, renewed their covenant vows, and pledged renewed faithfulness in the Christian life. This was truly an impressive and melting scene; the stillness of the grave prevailed, while the spirit of God was moving on the hearts of these enlisted veterans in the army of the Prince of Peace. Seeing the grace of God, we were glad and exhorted them all that with purpose of heart they would cleave unto the Lord.

"Evidently the Holy Spirit was striving with many of our hearers who had not abandoned the service of sin, and entered into the service of God. We earnestly appealed to such, and invited them now to set their heart to seek the Lord, and secure an interest in the Lamb of God that taketh away the sin of the world. Seven men, rising to their feet, inquired what they must do to be saved. After directing them to Christ, ready and willing to save, to the uttermost, the chief of sinners, I asked some brother soldier to lead in prayer in behalf of these precious souls. A private soldier who sat near me, bowed on his knees, and poured out his heart before God in fervent supplications for his comrades now seeking Jesus, that they might find salvation in His blood, realize its gracious power, and share its divine realities of blessedness and joy.

"At the close of these moments rich in blessing, these men, with others of the Christian Brotherhood, gathered around the desk. Grasping their hands, we bid them God-speed in the way of life, usefulness in the tent and camp, victory over every sin, and an abundant entrance into the better land above. Thus ended the labors of a delightful Sabbath—hours of worship and Christian fellowship never to be forgotten, sweet foretaste of that Sabbath which never ends, and that congregation never to break up. With the sailor articled to the Captian of our salvation, in the forecastle, or on the deck, we have enjoyed the sweet hour of prayer, of praise, and worship; so with the soldier true to his God and Saviour, in his tent on the field, or languishing in the hospital, we have found that

> " ' The men of grace have found
>   Glory begun below:
> Celestial fruit on earthly ground
>   From faith and hope may grow.'

" About three months elapsed, and the following letters revived the memories of that Sabbath and its precious hours:

"Fort Columbus, N. Y. Harbor, }
        Nov. 1, 1863.   }

" Rev. Brother:—I take the opportunity of writing you a few lines, for it seems to me that I owe you more than I shall ever be able to pay. I have seen you but two or three times, and I

may never see you again on earth, but I hope to
meet you in heaven. I am now a soldier of the
Cross, and a soldier of my country, and I hope I
shall never desert my colors. I told you that if
ever, by the grace of God, I reached heaven, it
was your hand that led me there. God bless
you, my dear Christian brother, and that is all
I can do for you, who, under God, has done so
much for me. I can write no more, for my
heart is full of joy.

   " Your friend,
      " A. H. "

" Having conversed with so many soldiers, I
had no distinct recollection of this man. I at
once addressed him a letter, and soon received
the following reply:

'Thanks for your kind letter. I will ex-
plain to you where I met you. It was at the
chapel in Camp Dennison, Ohio. I heard you
preach one Sunday. soon after the church was
opened, and I went to the prayer meeting, after
which you preached, and you gave an invitation for those who desired to serve God, to
stand up. I did so, and you may remember
that I took you by the hand and told you that
by the grace of God if I ever reached heaven,

your hand had led me there. I belong to the
regulars. Our Colonel is a soldier of the Cross,
and we hold prayer meetings three times a
week. I have a fact of interest to tell you.
With my other duties, I am sexton of our
chapel, and at first I used to sleep in the chapel.
One night, quite late, I awoke by hearing the
voice of prayer in the entry; I soon discovered
three persons there, I knew the voice of one
of them: it was Sergeant B——, who teaches
school for the drummer boys. They were not
a little surprised when I opened the door and
invited them in. I ascertained from Sergeant
B—— that they had been in New York city at
a prayer meeting. The Sergeant, by his influence, and the divine aid, had led these two
dear drummer boys to the feet of Jesus. After
prayer with them I bid them good night.

'Dear Brother, I am seeking for a closer
walk with God. Pray for me; the spirit is willing, but the flesh is weak. Pray for me that
God may fill my soul with holy courage, that I
may never yield to sin, that I may always stand
true to the banner of Jesus Christ. I want so
to live, that when I am about to die I may hear
the voice of Jesus say to me:

'Soldier of Christ, well done,
 Go forth from earth's employ;
The battle's fought, the victory won;
Enter thy Master's joy.'

'My prayers are often offered for you. God bless you, dear Christian friend, and all your labors of love. Your brother in Christ,

'A. H.'

"Our chapel was not built in vain. Within its walls sinners have been converted to God, and the faith of believers strengthened. Soldiers, sick and well, are found anxious to enjoy the means of grace. Faith made heroes of old. Joshua, Gideon and David were men of religious principles and devout life. General Havelock could pray in the jungles of India while hastening to the rescue of the beleaguered at Lucknow; Capt. Hedley Vicars, in the trenches of Sebastopol, honored his Christian profession by a godly life and triumphant faith. General Mitchell, the devout astronomer, the heroic soldier, witnessed for Jesus at the head of his victorious army, and the valiant Admiral Foote, with his officers and crew, bowed in prayer on the deck of his flag-ship on the eve of battle and of victory. The American soldier, true to

his manhood, his God and his country, may be
a valiant soldier of the Cross. Amid the trials
and temptations of the camp and the perils of
the battle-field, he may enjoy the life and power
of religion. Languishing from disease, or suffering from wounds, faith in Jesus is his un-
failing support and abounding consolation. Receiving from the icy hand of death his final discharge from the conflict of life, he will find it
endorsed, 'Good and faithful servant, enter
thou into the joy of thy Lord.'

"Ministering in the gospel of clean clothes,
soft pillows, nutritious food and religious consolation, among the wounded after the battle of
Perryville, Ky., the following incident occurred: In one of the village meeting-houses
where over a hundred of the victims of the battle-field were lying on the floor, two brave boys
had died the preceding night, and their bodies,
waiting for burial, were tenderly laid in a corner near the door and covered with a blanket.
Obtaining the consent of the faithful and devoted surgeon, I held a short religious service
in honor of the fallen heroes, and with the hope
of comforting their surviving comrades, some
of whom were evidently approaching life's last

hour and the vast eternity that lies a mysterious reality just beyond. As I spoke of that life and immortality brought to light in the gospel, and of Him who is the resurrection and the life, and who whispers in the ear of fainting humanity trusting in his power to save, 'Because I live, ye shall live also,' many bosoms moved with deep emotion, and eyes of brave men were filled with tears. On the left lay a wounded man with not many days to live, but evidently with a soul in full sympathy with hope beyond the grave.

"He struggled with his emotions, but the swelling tide could not be repressed. Bringing his hands together, he exclaimed, 'Glory to God for the hope of eternal life through Jesus Christ my Lord.'

"On those straw pallets were other sufferers ready to echo the same rapturous and glowing words, prompted by the same experience of Christ, made unto them of God, wisdom, right-eousness, sanctification, and redemption. At the close of our service I inquired of that dear brother as to the ground of his faith and his joy. 'Yes, I love Jesus; and He loves me,' was his prompt response and his blessed expe-

rience. Standing at the side of this soldier of
the Cross, now at the portals of death, waiting
orders from the Captain of his salvation, I could
but exclaim, 'Thanks be to God, which giveth
us the victory, through our Lord Jesus Christ,'
and to repeat in his ears those sweet words:

> ' In the furnace God will try thee,
>   Thence to bring thee forth more bright;
> He can never cease to love thee,
>   Thou art precious in his sight.'

"In making my way to the door, passing between two rows of sufferers, I felt some one
pull at my coat. I turned around, and a poor
fellow said, 'Preacher, are you in a hurry?'
'No, my friend; what do you wish?' 'Well,
I am not like John, over there; he is ready to
die, and knows what is to become of him after
death. I am not like him; tell me, Oh tell me
what I must do to be saved?' Poor man, he
had neglected his soul's salvation and the Bible;
deep darkness brooded over his awakened mind;
and he was evidently honestly and earnestly inquiring the way to be saved. Blessed privilege
to tell him of Jesus, the sinner's friend—of the
salvation of the dying thief on the cross, who
trusted Him. The prayer of the publican,

'God, be merciful to me, a sinner,' filled his soul, and found utterance from his lips—and who can doubt that it reached the ears of our merciful and faithful High Priest, 'who can have compassion on the ignorant, and them that are out of the way.' Soldier, reader, if your sin is a burden on your soul; if you are in the dark, go to the mercy-seat and tell Jesus; go just now; go just as you are. All the fitness he requireth is to feel your need of Him.

"On board of a steamer passing down the Ohio river, was a detachment of troops on their way to the front. On the guards of the boat, separated from his comrades, I observed a young soldier seated on a box reading a Testament. It was a very pleasant sight, and with emotions of deep interest my eye rested on the attentive reader. In a little time a soldier approached the youth, rudely removing his cap, and words of ridicule and derision fell from his lips. I trembled for the soldier-boy, and a silent prayer was offered in his behalf, that the thoughtless indignity and ridicule of his comrade might not overcome his integrity in the hour of provocation and trial.

"The young soldier bore it all with meekness, made no resentment, but quietly regaining his place on the box, resumed the reading of his precious book.

" There was the true hero, and moral courage of the purest type! In the hour of temptation he maintained his integrity and dared to do right. His conduct deeply impressed my mind. In a few moments I approached the dear youth, laid my hand on his shoulder, and with a few kind words of Christian sympathy made his acquaintance. He told me of a pious and faithful mother, and of Sabbath-school instruction; that he loved the Word of God, and had taken it for the guide of his youth. I told him that with trembling solicitude I had watched his conduct when rudely treated and ridiculed by his comrade—that I greatly admired his unflinching firmness, his gentleness and triumph. He replied in these touching words: 'Oh yes, I could stand all that, for I was doing what my mother told me to do; that I must not let a day pass without reading the Word of God, and thinking about my soul.' Thus taught of his beloved mother, this soldier-boy, faithful to those godly teachings, was well prepared to meet temptations and to maintain his integrity.

" Brave youth! the Lord God of the armies of Israel keep thee in the hollow of his hand, and abundantly reward thy godly mother, whose words of truth were so deeply engraved on thy manly heart."

F

CHAPTER VII.

RESIGNATION OF CHAPLAINCY.

———

M R. CHIDLAW'S very extended and efficient labors as a Chaplain were eventually interrupted by the failure of his health,

By advice of army surgeons he resigned his
Chaplaincy; at his age (then about 50), the exposure of active service had undermined his
strength. One who knew him well, writes:
"Of all the men of our acquaintance, he seemed
the best fitted by nature and grace for that important duty. But when we remembered his
comparatively frail physique, we feared much
that he would only last to enter upon his work."
He retired North; but his restless nature could
not long brook inactivity. Having regained his
health, he resumed his public labors in behalf
of the Sunday-school cause, and, with pen and
tongue, exerted himself in defence of the
Union.

Such notices as these frequently appeared in
the papers:

ARMY MEETING

FOR THE

SOLDIERS IN THE HOSPITAL AND FREEDMEN OF THE SOUTH.

Rev. B. W. Chidlaw, Missionary of the A. S. S. Union, and late Chaplain in the U. S. Army in Missouri, will give his experience of Camp Life among the Soldiers, at the New England Church, South 9th Street, Brooklyn, N. Y., on Thursday evening, May 15th, commencing at 7:45 o'clock. Every one that loves his country, and its brave suffering soldiers, should hear this veteran and eloquent Missionary relate his story. It abounds in narratives of thrilling interest.

A Collection will be taken for the benefit of the sick and wounded Soldiers, to be expended by Rev. Mr. Chidlaw, who expects soon to return to his work among the Hospitals in the West and South."

(From the *New York Observer.*)

"That devoted, heroic Chaplain of an Ohio regiment, Rev. Mr. Chidlaw, was in the meeting. His regiment is at Pittsburgh Landing, or beyond, lying in front of the enemy. He said that some time last summer he spent weeks and

months among the Ohio regiments as a missionary—a volunteer—doing good as he had opportunity. At length he had a regular appointment
as Chaplain, and he had been with his 'boys'
until his health broke down, and he was compelled to leave for a season to recruit it.

"He told of sickness and death which he had
witnessed in the camp.   *   *   *   One man
died, saying he had never read a chapter in the
Bible in his life, never had attended a place of
public worship on the Sabbath; and when entering the dark valley of the shadow of death,
he sent for the Chaplain, saying in his own
Western language that 'he was powerfully afraid
to die.' The man was from Missouri. And he
died uttering his fears.

"He spoke of another young man, who had
been a Sunday-school scholar.   *   *   *
'How do you feel about dying?" asked the Chaplain. 'Oh!' answered the lad, 'I am ready, I
am not afraid to die. I believe in Jesus, He
is my trust and I commit my all to Him. I am
not afraid to die,' And in a joyful state the
poor lad passed away from our view."

(From a Western Paper.)

"While in the city I met Mr. Chidlaw, the

famous Sunday-school man, my college-mate and early Christian friend, to whom as Christ's servant I owe much for the type of my early life. He heard my rapid story, handed me $3, promised a larger sum hereafter and his intercessions when they may be worth to us thousands a few years hence, and, just like him, the next minute was out of sight."

That the ordinarily serious Welshman could appreciate humor upon occasion may be inferred from this bit of army news, which the patriotic soul doubtless greatly enjoyed retailing:

" Rev. B. W. Chidlaw, who has just returned from Nashville, says that he saw marching through the streets of that city, a company of some fifty or more soldiers, in night caps. They were called the ' Night Cap Brigade.' They had been disgraced for delivering themselves up to the enemy in order to get home on parole. The caps were made of cotton cloth, and had large frills."

CHAPTER VIII.

———

OUT of the exigencies of the war and the necessities of our brave men at the front, as is well-known, grew the beneficent organization termed the "Sanitary Commission." Mr. Chidlaw's sympathies were naturally early enlisted in its behalf; and when debarred from engaging further in the work of the army chaplainship, upon the partial restoration of his health, he became increasingly and heartily involved in these generous ministries to the bodily needs of the men at the front, as will appear from a series of letters from his pen:

"CINCINNATI, June 18, 1862.

"The hospitals in the city are not much crowded now. They are in a good condition, and a poor invalid soldier is well cared for. Through the kindness of friends I have suspended the 'Silent Comforter' on their walls, and the eyes of many have thereby read of Christ, and hope and heaven. At Camp Dennison, 12 miles out of the city, I found ample provisions to meet the wants of the sick and wounded. Here was a mother watching a dying son; both rejoiced in Christ as their personal Saviour, and tenderly spoke of his love. This mother told me that her husband, another son, and a son-in-law were in the army; she thanked God that she had such a family, loyal to Christ and loyal to their country, and that Divine grace sustained her in this day of trial and bereavement. With her kind hand she wiped the brow of her soldier boy, and bedewed his couch with her tears, but murmured not a word."

"St. Louis, Mo., June 20, 1862.

" In spending a few days in the hospitals, introducing the 'Silent Comforter,' and other good reading, conversing with the afflicted, praying at the bedside of the dying, and holding religious service among the convalescents, the surgeons, stewards and nurses afforded me every facility I could wish, and frequently expressed a sympathy with my labors which cheered my heart.

"On leaving a ward, after hanging up the 'Silent Comforter,' and conversing with several of the sufferers, a nurse told me, 'A man wants you to talk to him.' I returned, found a

young man very low, evidently on the crumbling verge of time. His respiration was difficult and he whispered feebly, ' I cannot talk
much. Speak to me of Jesus Christ and pray
for me.' His eye was bright, his mind un-
clouded, and his face beamed with smiles, while
I talked of Him whom his soul loved, the sinner's friend, death's destroyer, and eternal life.

" Another sufferer with whom I had conversed
and prayed, said. ' It is a blessed thing to die
looking up.' I inquired, 'And what does my
soldier brother behold?' ' Christ and heaven,'
was his prompt and enthusiastic reply."

" PERRYVILLE, Nov. 13, 1862.

" In a ward where I left ten hymn books, a
convalescent soldier said, ' Boys, this is just
what we want, we can now sing the hymns we
used to at home.' Clean clothes, soft pillows,
and kind words, are just the introduction we
need as ministers of Christ to carry our books
and to preach the Gospel in the wards of our
hospitals.

" The battle-field,—two miles from Perryville, where fifty to sixty thousand men met on
the 8th of October, in deadly conflict, and in less
than six hours 7,000 were killed or wounded—

was visited in company with an officer who had participated in the fight. Evidences of frightful carnage were seen, on entering the field of death, in hundreds of graves, trees, fences, houses and barns riddled with the missiles of death, the decaying carcasses of horses, wreck of batteries, accoutrements and clothing which strewed the field.

"While passing over the battle-field, we were told that some forty of our severely wounded men were at the Antioch Hospital, three miles off. Here we saw these brave, patient, uncomplaining men almost every one having suffered amputation. I promised to relieve them, and held religious services, in which they engaged with evident interest. Fifty had been buried from this hospital since the battle, and, I fear, several others cannot recover. From Perryville I sent them, through the kindness of the Cleveland ladies, who had supplies, dried apples, onions, potatoes, chocolate, etc.; and from the remnants of the twenty-eight boxes in my charge at Lebanon, I hope to send them canned fruit, clothing, and books which will meet their present wants.

"The thousands of soldiers now in our hospitals, in the wake of the great army of the west, have strong claims upon our earnest and generous efforts to mitigate their sufferings, and save their precious lives. The Christian and Sanitary Commissions need and must have our aid in the relief of those noble men who have imperiled their all for us. Government medical supplies are provided, but this is not all that the afflicted soldier needs. The kind hearts and willing hands of our wives, mothers and sisters must meet this necessity. They must have money to purchase yarn, flannel, sheeting, etc. We, the husbands, fathers, brothers and friends must furnish them with the material and the work will be done well and promptly."

"New York, Jan. 30, 1863.

"The state of the country is trying men's souls. Timid people, and those absorbed in the pursuit of gain and devoted to pleasure, are showing weakness in the knees. Rebel sympa· thizers cry peace, peace, but afford no practical plan, or a gleam of hope to preserve the Union, and maintain the government. Pro-slaveryism sees nothing but ruin, if the peculiar institution is not sacredly preserved. But the masses

of the people have faith in God, and are determined to crush the rebellion at all hazards."

Rev. Mr. Chidlaw then describes a regiment
recruited under circumstances of more than
ordinary interest.

"ST. LOUIS, Mo., March 23.

"The 37th Regiment Iowa Volunteer Infantry is made up of men *over forty-five years
old*, and is now quartered in Schofield Barracks
in this city, doing provost duty. Two of its
members are over eighty years old, hale, noble
looking veterans, and good for hard service.
About 600 are members of Christian churches;
twenty-eight are ministers of the gospel; all the
staff officers are religious men. Most of these
veterans left farms and comfortable homes, and
have sons and grandsons in the service. One
of these members, evidently hard on to the
seventieth mile-stone in life's journey, and looking rather feeble—when I suggested that he
would need a discharge from the service, the
old man straightened up, the fires of youth
flashing from his eyes, and said: 'No, sir; I
enlisted to fight rebels and to crush rebellion,
and not to be discharged till the work is done.
I quit playing baby fifty years ago, when I was

twenty-one years old;' adding, 'I am in earnest for God and my country.'

"On Sunday, the writer was invited to hold divine service in their barracks. At the appointed hour the 'Grey-Beards,' in their neat and clean uniforms, truly soldier-like, officers and privates, gathered around him, and heard with fixed attention the words of eternal life. This remarkable regiment is an honor to the State of Iowa, to their own manhood and the glorious cause for which they are willing to live, suffer and to die. God bless the veterans of Iowa."

Rev. Mr. Chidlaw's addresses were a very potent factor in arousing and shaping public opinion as to the great issues and grave responsibilities of the war. As a fearless, outspoken loyalist none excelled him. People never wearied of hearing this man of God. Wherever he went he was received with cordiality and heard with enthusiasm. The high and influential quality of his address was attested by many press notices, such as the following:

"The army meeting Sabbath evening * * * is anticipated with much interest. * * * Rev. B. W. Chidlaw, of Cincinnati, has been one of those Chaplains that have secured the love of his regiment, and the confidence and respect of all who know him. He never fails to interest his audience."

Sheridan said of Rowland Hill: "I always love to hear Hill, for the words come red-hot from his heart." So we and all may feel concerning our friend, the soldier's friend, and everybody's friend—Rev. B. W. Chidlaw.

The man and his oratory were well described by such paragraphs as these from the public press:

"For more than half a century Rev. B. W. Chidlaw has been the Presbyterian Moody of the Ohio Valley. Welsh-born, he inherited the Christmas Evans style of energy and eloquence."

"If Rev. Mr. Chidlaw were to rise in an audience now, where he was unknown, nobody in that audience would need to be told that somebody had the floor."

"He is still Chidlaw—that is to say, one of the most *provoking* men you ever heard. You cannot hear him without feeling that you are a slow coach, that you must jump round and pitch in."

This last assertion finds an echo in a refer·
ence in the *Religious Telescope*, where he
is alluded to as "the indefatigable, the irrepressible Chidlaw, whose praise is in all the
churches, and who has energy enough to
set a dozen common men spinning like a top."

At a large and enthusiastic army meeting
held in St. Louis, March 24, 1863, Mr. Chidlaw announced as the subject of his remarks:
"The Army and Navy as Fields of Philanthropic and Christian Efforts."

He referred to these fields as new and peculiar, wide and important, often difficult, but
always hopeful and encouraging. The development and culture of the moral and religious
elements in the service were urgently pressed
by facts and arguments. Good men made
good soldiers and sailors. Good principles,
foundation stones of truth in the soul, secure
integrity, true loyalty and unflinching bravery.

Faith in God, he said, made heroes of old,
and so it will now. Hedley Vicars, in the
siege of Sebastopool, and Henry Havelock, in
the jungles of India, were men of strong religious principles and godly life. "Fight for the
flag, and live by the Cross," is a glorious power

in our great struggle for national life, and it will surely win. The appliances for the development and strengthening of the religious elementi n the army were then presented. The official agency—the chaplainship, and the voluntary—the Sanitary and Christian commissions, were unfolded in their power and adaptation. He dwelt at length upon the work, the difficulties and results of the labors of chaplains who were adapted for and fully devoted to their true mission in the camp, on the field, and at the hospital. He had seen and addressed ten thousand noble soldiers invited to Divine worship by the distinguished presiding officer (Major-General Curtis) when in command at Benton Barracks. Religious and miscellaneous reading the soldiers always appreciated and thankfully received. The brave soldier, imperriling his life for his country and his Government, does not become an outcast— does not necessarily ignore the teachings of his youth, or desert the altars around which his parents taught him to revere and worship God.

Patriotism and religion impel us to the duty of providing for the spiritual as well as the physical wants of the soldier and sailor. The Church of Christ, the true religious sentiment of the land. must give power and efficacy to the labors of the Christian Commission—then the soldier will feel that magnetic influence which thrills his soul, and tells him that he has strong, earnest and reliable friends in his rear.

Rev. Mr. Chidlaw closed his remarks in an urgent appeal for aid, referring to an ancient medal with an ox standing between the plow and an altar, encircled with this inscription: 'Ready for either—to toil at the plow or bleed on the altar.' In suppressing this wicked and gigantic rebellion, he said feelingly: "In vindicating and sustaining the authority of the Government, we must partake of this self-sacrificing and heroic spirit. A million of noble hearts are ready to bleed on the altar—thousands have already bled, martyrs in a glorious and holy cause. Let us who stay home, toil and suffer, that the brave men—the living wall between us and the uplifted arm of treason, madly, wickedly assailing all that is dear in our homes, our sanctuaries, our laws and our Government, let us have faith in God, faith in each other, faith in the Government, and soon peace and union will bless our land."

This address was one of his happiest efforts

—earnest, Christian, patriotic, and overflowing with love to the sufferers; and to Him who has shed His precious blood for them.

At its close Gen. Strong was introduced. He said, " I asked the chairman of the Army Committee who is to speak?" " Rev. B. W. Chidlaw," was the reply. "Then," said I, " You have enough, and, (turning to the audience), have you not had?"

We continue the story in Mr. Chidlaw's words:

" MEMPHIS, April 20, ——.

" We arrived here on Saturday, discharged stores for the hospitals here and at Corinth, and tied up for the Sabbath.

" In the hospitals, which are in a very good condition, are nearly 1.000 inmates, and in the convalescent camp within Fort Pickering, an equal number. Here we found that books and tracts were much needed and eagerly sought after. The work of distribution over, and the last rays of the Sabbath sun falling on us athwart the smooth surface of the " Father of Waters," we selected an open space in the midst of the tents, and commenced preaching Jesus to a few who surrounded us, and in a few moments a large crowd attentively heard the message of

G

salvation; and at the close, gratefully acknowledged their appreciation of this small token of
interest in their spiritual welfare."

"Yesterday,—Sabbath—at an early hour,
mounted on a 'charger,' through the kindness
of a friend, I visited the beautiful camp of the
5th Ohio Cavalry. Lieutenant-Colonel Heath
gave me a very cordial welcome. The boys
soon gathered around me, and we had a good
time in greeting old acquaintances and forming
new ones. Cleves, Miamitown, and Elizabethtown were well represented by a noble and sol-
dierly band of men.   *   *   *   Col. Taylor
was not in the camp, but at the invitation of
Lieutenant-Colonel Heath, we talked to the men
on religion and patriotism, and gave them
'something good to read.' The boys are 'powerfully' down on copperhead peace-mongers at
home, and wish all their true friends to know
it. The gallant 5th O. V. C. is all right; the
dash of their charges, the heavy blows of their
sabres, and their well-aimed carbines, will, as
heretofore, tell the traitors in the front and
rear, their devotion to the old flag and the Government in the hour of peril."

(Describing a convalescent camp, two miles

below Milliken's Bend on a fine plantation,) he says:

YOUNG'S POINT, LA., April 26.

" The planter's mansion surrounded with blooming magnolias, fragrant vines, and beautiful flowers; the overseer's house, the quarters, and a line of tents, were occupied by about thirteen hundred of our brave men—cheerful, and most of them rapidly recovering. As we discharged our cargo, hundreds of hearts throbbed with joy, as they felt that they were not forgotten by friends at home. In one of the quarters neat and comfortable, occupied by twenty or twenty-five men, while distributing reading matter, one of the men with a full heart said: ' Bless God for what you are doing. You feed the body and the soul. That is what we need. Thank God for friends at home!'

" This encampment is in sight of Vicksburg. A few nights ago, six transports ran the blockade; one was wrecked, the others landed nearly 600,000 rations. The belching of a hundred cannons was terrific, and made the earth tremble. On one of the boats, the framework on which the pilot stood—(Ab. Karns, of the 30th O. V. I., who volunteered his services)—was torn to

pieces by a ball, but the brave soldier re-ar-
ranged the fragments, and stood at the wheel,
but in a few moments a deadly missile cut him
in pieces. Another kindred spirit grasped the
wheel, and continued the transport on her
course.

" Near Milliken's Bend, in a very large camp—
(Gen. Logan's division,)—I was invited to hold
religious service, and with two fellow laborers,
Brothers Brunell and Reynolds, preached the
precious Gospel of Jesus Christ to two brigades.
The sun was declining behind the gorgeous
forest trees in our rear; two immense congregations were assembled; in the centre of these circles of upturned heads, with a supply of publications for distribution, we stood in the name
of our exalted Master, and spoke His precious
words of love and salvation to these vast assemblies, who were under marching orders and
approaching the frowning batteries of an entrenched enemy.   *   *   *   Chaplains in
the field have, at best, a trying and difficult position; they need the real sympathy of the churches
and ministers. Let us do something to help
them. Write to them, sending them reading
matter, and visit them at their post of duty.

In the Revolutionary struggle, our Wither-spoons, our Caldwells, our Duffields, our Bishop Whites, represented the Church of Christ, and why should not our ministers leave their high places on the walls of Zion at home and go to the front, among our brave but exposed soldiers? Much depends on the development and culture of the religious element in the army, and the American Church has no higher mission to-day, than awaits it in our immense army; here its highest ministerial gifts, its richest experience and liberal contributions, will find a work which God will approve and bless."

"Young's Point, La., May 4, 1863.

"From Cairo, Ill., to this place, a distance of six hundred miles, most of the plantations on both sides of the river are abandoned and desolate. No furrow upturned, no growing corn or cotton did we see; fences gone by flood or fire, houses and quarters destroyed, and all a perfect waste. In the interior, to a fearful extent, the same sad condition exists. My heart sickens at the sight of these terrible devastations and sufferings, the inevitable result of the madness and wickedness of the slave power to destroy the best Government ever known. "Surely the way of the transgressor is hard."

"The treason of the master having removed the manacles of the slave, thousands are now boldly and nobly striking for their freedom, not by deeds of violence and blood, but orderly and quietly. On the banks of the river we frequently saw groups of these panting fugitives, men, women and children, with their 'little all,' anxiously waiting deliverance. Government transports receive them, and they are taken to such places as the United States Commissioners select, where they are furnished with rations, and find employment on abandoned plantations. If they fall into the hands of humane, honest, energetic and God-fearing employers, are taught habits of industry and economy, instructed in the Christian faith and morals, supplied with implements of husbandry, food and clothing (earned by their labor), their freedom will be a blessing to themselves and to their country. Everything depends upon their proper management at this critical period of their transition from bondage to freedom. Set to work promptly, and kindly directed, they can raise corn and cotton in abundance; but the season is passing, and I fear that the tardiness and inefficiency of officials in whose charge they are, will result in grievous injury to these poor people, and render their support a serious burden to the Government. Help them to help themselves, afford them protection, teach them self-reliance, and all will be right."

Rev. Mr. Chidlaw's unfeigned interest in the colored people is evident from this letter, written from Young's Point, May 4th, 1863:

"At Milliken's Bend three transports yesterday afternoon landed three thousand contrabands from plantations in the rear of Greenville, Miss. They camped on the levee, and such a scene we never witnessed. It beggars description. All were busy and cheerful; some receiving rations, some kindling fires, and others arranging old tents and boards into a shelter and a temporary home. I spent hours among them, found many who love Jesus, and would know more about his love and power to save; docile as little children, they were anxious to receive instruction. I heard no profanity among them, and all their conduct was decorous and commendable. One poor fellow, loud in his expressions of joy that he was free,

said, 'We owe dis to de broklamation of de
President of dese United States.' An older
man, with great seriousness, added, 'But de
Lord had de biggest hand in it.' Very many
of these people are religious, but in great need
of instruction. Late in the evening several
groups held worship. Their singing and prayers were very impressive. The religious and
social elevation of these people, God's poor at
our doors, is a work of love and mercy earnestly appealing to the church of Christ. Here
is a missionary work worthy of the immediate
and earnest efforts of every Christian and patriotic heart in the land. Providence has never
opened a more interesting and encouraging
missionary field. Already there is a strong religious element among them—their language is
ours, and elementary books of instruction and
the Bible we have in abundance. All things
are ready. Shall we take Ethiopia's out-
stretched hand and fill it with Gospel blessings,
and by Christian influences elevate and cheer
these down-trodden people ? The hour and opportunity are come; we have it in our power to
honor God, bless our country, and save these
perishing people."

"Two weeks ago, when distributing books
and tracts on the U. S. Floating Hospital
' Nashville,' at Milliken's Bend, La., a feeble
voice uttered my name. This brought me to
the cot of a young man, feeble and emaciated.
He was the son of an old friend in Delaware
Co., Ohio, a member of the 96th regiment
O. V. I., a Christian soldier, a youth of talent
and promise. Enquiring into his religious experience and enjoyment on the bed of languishing, with a placid smile he replied, '*I am happy
day and night; Jesus is my all in all.*' We
bowed at his cot and besought the Lord on his
behalf, giving thanks to the God of all grace
and consolation, that our afflicted friend dwelt
under the shadow of a great rock, rejoicing in
tribulation, and filled with peace."

"While in the South, a few days since, where
the Negroes are rapidly enlisting, I addressed
one of them,

"Well, soldier, you are going to fight for
your country ?"

"Yes, massa."

"Do you think the Lord will take care of
you ?"

"Don't *tink* nothing about it, massa; I *know*
he will.' "

CHAPTER IX.

———

A MAN like Dr. Chidlaw could not fail to be deeply interested in such an enterprise as the U. S. Christian Commission. His clear conception of its true aim and method, is evidenced by an address delivered at a public meeting in Philadelphia.

After alluding to the Providence of God as manifested in the war, the speaker said: "It is a wonderful fact, my hearers, in our history, that we present the first instance of the organization of a patriotic philanthropic association, to send bodily relief and spiritual comfort to soldiers in the field. From the time when David was sent to his brethren in the camp—the first delegate of the Christian Commission—with the loaves and cheese for their comfort, no great national effort has been made to relieve the necessities of men in arms.

"The Christian Commission, in the combination of relief for the body and consolation for the soul, is at once the good Samaritan and the true Evangelist, and as such, commends itself to every Christian and philanthropic heart."

Returning to Philadelphia from a tour in behalf of the U. S. Christian Commission in northeastern Pennsylvania, Rev. Mr. Chidlaw wrote that the uprising of the people in its glorious reality was everywhere evident. "The train from Easton was crowded with the stalwart men of North Jersey, hastening to the rescue. Chestnut Street appeared like one continued recruiting office, with an immense business going on. Stores, shops and manufactories were pouring out their thousands of strong men ready to meet the invader. At Wilkesbarre and Scranton, the hardy miners heard the call to arms, and dropped their picks to shoulder their muskets. At the latter place our Christian Commission service was turned into a war meeting, and the next morning some 200 heroic men were on the train, and amid deafening cheers were off for the war. The men of New York, New Jersey and the Keystone State blending in mighty masses, with shouts as of victorious hosts, passed the Old Hall of Independence, and catching the inspirations of '76 made their way amid loud cheers and thousands of waving handkerchiefs to the depot of the Pennsylvania Railroad. There is no panic or fear, but one outburst of enthusiasm and strengthened confidence in the results of this great struggle for national life and unity,"

Rev. Mr. Chidlaw's work in September carried him South again—this time to Alabama—where, at Stevenson, September 27th, he was "discovered" by a correspondent of a northern paper, and thus described to its readers: "While floundering about through the suffocating dust of this place this morning, I discovered a moving pillar of mother earth, on the summit of which I recognized the features of Rev. Mr. Chidlaw, of Cincinnati. He is here with thirteen others on behalf of the Christian Commission, which has been doing a noble work in ministering to the wants of the wounded, as they have passed through to Chattanooga. They have fed and clothed thousands of the poor and suffering fellows, and are entitled to a nation's gratitude for their labor of love. The work is truly philanthropic, and should be aided by every friend of the soldier and lover of the cause." But let Mr. Chidlaw tell the story in his own words:

" STEVENSON, ALA., Sept. 25, 1863.

" On Wednesday noon, with twelve fellow-
laborers, we left Cincinnati, and on Thursday
night reached Nashville. Here we found that
1,300 wounded soldiers from Chattanooga had
arrived and another 100 was expected. * * *
To-day, at the request of our excellent field-
agent, brother Parsons, I was appointed to supply the wounded men that arrive from the front.
Colonel Lyon, Post Commander, gave me a detail of twenty-four men, and a large tent near
the railroad depot. In this we have our food,
and near by a fire, with fifteen large camp kettles,
coffee and sugar. When a train arrives, the
sufferers from the field of battle, exhausted and
hungry, are promptly furnished with food, and
we are abundantly repaid by their grateful acknowledgments."

" STEVENSON, ALA., Oct. 1, 1863.

" Since the last battle near Chattanooga.
twenty delegates of the United States Christian Commission have reported here. Ten
have passed on, and ten of us are here on duty.
Our home is an unfinished meeting house.

" Yesterday, a brother in his blue coat stood
up to tell of his struggles and trials in the Chris-

tian life, and said with feeling, 'Brethren, after
all, and in all these dark times, by the grace of
God I am Jesus Christ's enlisted man, under His
banner there can be no defeat, but certain
victory."

"Another aged soldier, testifying of the grace
of God, the love of Jesus, and the power of
faith, said, 'I have seen hard times, long
marches, great dangers, and sometimes felt that
I must fall out of the ranks, but just then, when
so weak and faint, I would look to God, think
of the end of my pilgrimage, and the crown of
glory beyond, I would jog on and feel strong.
My brethren, religion greatly helps the soldier,
soul and body!' *   *   * We distributed
150 sheets of paper, and the same number of
envelopes. This small favor was opportune and
highly appreciated. A young soldier—shot in
the foot, quite a sufferer,—said: 'How glad my
mother will be to hear from me, now that I
have paper to write home!' In writing for
these patient, uncomplaining men, I observed
the wide difference between the man that loves
Jesus and the man that knows Him not. The
former would tell his wife, sister, father or
friend, how precious his Saviour was to his soul,

what peace he enjoyed, how he was cheered and sustained in the hour of danger and in his present sufferings. The other has no such message to send, no words of comfort and of hope for his loved ones at home. The old soldier was certainly right when he said ' religion greatly helps the soldier, soul and body,' and it is a special comfort to the friends at home to know that the soldier sick and well, has Christ for his all in all."

"NASHVILLE, TENN., Oct. 3, 1863.

"After laboring a week at Stevenson and Bridgeport, Ala., among the sick, wounded and well soldiers, in the camps and hospitals, we reached this city at noon to-day.   *   *   *
We found many Ohio soldiers here, quite cheerful and thankful for our words of cheer and religious reading. We learn that about 5,000 wounded men are now in the Nashville hospitals. Half of them are slightly wounded, and will soon return to duty. We heard none complaining. Many express great anxiety to join their comrades in front. Arrangements are made for all the delegates, both lay and clerical, to labor to-morrow among the teamsters, detached regiments in the fortification and at the various hos-

pitals. How much we need the unction from above, and the love of Christ inspiring our hearts—amid these various and important labors! Brethren, pray for us and come over and help us!"

He advocated organized effort on a large scale in a speech before the American Tract Society:

"The few minutes which I shall occupy will permit me but to glance at the view expressed in the language of the resolution, that the American Tract Society is justified in the expenditure of $30,000 in circulating amid the great army of soldiers throughout this land this precious Christian literature. We are justified in the fact that our army and navy needed these leaves of the tree of life, needed the blessed book that has God for its author, salvation for its end, and truth without the any mixture of, error; and blessed be God, the American Bible Society has never ceased with a liberal hand and a warm heart to supply the great army with the Word of eternal life. Religious reading for the soldier is greatly needed; 'for amid the toils and duties of camp-life, idleness is a grievous evil.' * * * I have found in my experience large numbers of men who could not read, larger numbers still who were not disposed to read such books as I presented to them. These men I could but very imperfectly reach; but the great mass of our western soldiers were anxious to receive a tract or book, and they were careful to preserve what was given them.

"As an evidence of this, one morning I saw a regiment that I had supplied with the Testament and the Soldiers' Hymn Book, slinging on their knapsacks and forming into line. I was afraid they might leave behind them a considerable portion of what I had given them, and I passed along the vacated cantonments, gathering up what books I could find—but very few were left. Our American soldiers, to a great extent, will read, and they love to read, these Christian publications that you furnish to them.

"This expenditure by the Tract Society has proved an invaluable aid in their pastoral duties to the 400 chaplains represented in the American army; and where, under the blue sky of heaven, has ever an army been favored with such a band of faithful, spiritual and devoted men? What an unexampled event in our history the genius of the Government and the spirit of

H

our Christianity sending out 400 pastors to the tented field and the hospitals of our country!

" I have seen men casting clover-seed on the snow, a hopeless kind of work as it seemed at the time; but I have passed by the same fields the following spring, and have seen them covered with a luxuriant crop of clover. This good seed that we are scattering over the length and breadth of the land in the east, west, north, and we trust at the south, will spring up and bring forth fruit to the honor and glory of God.

" Havelock and Vicars were men of faith; Foote and Mitchell in our western department were men that stood up for Jesus.

" This religious element in the army is the assurance that we shall bye and bye see, not a faded field of blue with stars gone down in darkness, but one with stars shining bright, cheerful and lustrous as ever.   This religious element in the army is our hope, this work of the benevolent societies in scattering the word of God and a Christian literature tends to strengthen it.

" Soon this dreadful war will end—God hasten the day!

" While many of our noble army will bite the ground in the agonies of death, and will never

again see their prairie dwellings or log cabins in
the far West, tens and hundreds of thousands,
their duties over, will again return to their
homes. What kind of men shall they be then?
Shall they be pure men? Men with unscathed
consciences, and of unsullied purity? They may
come home crippled, and with scars of honor
obtained upon many a battlefield; but shall they
come bankrupt in character? Shall they come
home with polluted lips, with intemperate and
profligate habits sweeping them down to des-
truction? Oh! May God forbid it. Christian
men, come to the rescue, and forbid it. Send
to the army your messengers of salvation, send
them the words of eternal life in these precious
books, in your prayers remember them before
God."

"On the evening of Sept. 4th, 1864, at Ply-
mouth, Ohio, Rev. Mr. Chidlaw addressed a
union meeting held in one of the churches,
speaking most eloquently and feelingly for about
an hour in behalf of the U. S. C. C., after which
a liberal collection was taken up for the purposes of the Commission. From an account of
the proceedings we quote the following:

"It added not a little to the interest of the

occasion that a company of volunteers, some eighty strong, under Capt. Jenkins, from Jackson county, were present on their way to Ironton, to be mustered into the service. They had come down on the cars Saturday evening, and waited here over the Sabbath. Instead of the rowdyism and drunkenness so common under such circumstances, they met and had preaching in their own language, and in the evening they gathered in front of their quarters and engaged in singing some of their spiritual songs in their native tongue. They were Welshmen, and most, if not all, were members of the Church.

"On invitation they came in a body to the church at 7:30 o'clock, and listened with interest to the facts and statements made by their fellow countrymen, Brother Chidlaw, in behalf of the soldiers in the army.

"At the close of the exercises, he addressed a few words of good cheer and timely advice to them as to their duties, which they will remember to their dying day. They also sang one of their Christian songs. The audience was very large and appreciative, and many eyes were wet with tears at the narrative of what is being done for our noble boys in the army by the Christian and Sanitary Commissions. It was a good day, and all felt it was good to be there.

" By the faithful labors of the delegates of the Commission, our brothers now, almost invariably, receive the good things for soul and body, sent to them by their friends. These delegates work gratuitously, and are persons acting only from love of doing good to the needy. There are more than a thousand ' Nightingales ' in this blessed work."

Life at one of the hospital centres at the front in the work of the U. S. C. C. is graphically portrayed in the subjoined sketch, from Rev. Mr. Chidlaw's pen:

" There is a large porch looking out into this garden. Here some of the delegates take their place every morning to lead our family worship, while the others arrange themselves around the garden. After worship they fall in line, and marching up to the kitchen receive a plate with a piece of pork and ' hard-tack,' and then going to a window a little further on get a cup of coffee. Each one gets a seat wherever he can on the ground, or standing, eats his rations. This is the way in which the delegates live.

"Coming out from the door, I met a Doctor of Divinity with his coat off, his shirt-sleeves rolled up, carrying a large kettle of farina, with a haversack on his shoulders, loaded with fruits, on his way to distribute to the sick and wounded soldiers.

" When the labors of the day draw to a close, the delegates assemble in the garden and hold a prayer meeting. These are the most deeply interesting meetings I have ever attended.

" I found the organization of the work here very complete, and well systematized. The delegates are divided into companies, with a delegate experienced in former battle-fields for a captain. These are assigned to the various hospitals. Each delegate reports to his Captain, and the captains to the general field agent daily."

The quality of the men who ministered in the hospitals may be judged of by a single case mentioned by Mr. Chidlaw, who reported with regard to one establishment:

" I became acquainted with a ward master, a soldier belonging to the 1st E. Tenn. Cavalry, a most godly and patriotic man. In Hawkins Co., Tennessee, he was pastor of four Baptist churches, all loyal. With the male members of his churches, he was compelled to leave his home, his wife and four children, and the pastoral care of these churches. Wandering among the mountains for a week, in great peril and suffering, he reached our lines and enlisted. Health failed, and this good brother, with Christian faithfulness, is now doing a good work for the souls and bodies of the sick and wounded in the hospitals."

COMMITTEE'S REPORT OF THE CINCINNATI BRANCH OF THE UNITED STATES CHRISTIAN COMMISSION, JAN. 1, 1864.

"GEO. H. STUART, ESQ., Pres. U. S. Christian Commission:

"The Cincinnati Branch of the U. S. Christian Commission was organized early last summer. At our first public meeting, Gen. Burnside favored us with an address, and our friends gave us the first collection in behalf of the Commission. Since that time we have received $21,250 in cash, besides a large amount of stores and publications. We have sent forty-eight delegates to the field, the camp and the hospitals of the armies of Generals Grant and Burnside. Thirty-six are now at work for Christ and our country. During the year I traveled eighteen thousand six hundred miles, and made one hundred and fifty addresses in behalf of the Commission. My labors have extended into Missouri, Arkansas, Louisiana, Tennessee, Kentucky and Alabama. I have always been welcomed by officers and privates, and my labors gratefully appreciated. In his tent, or lingering in his cot, the soldier, sick or well, gladly received the benefactions of friends at home, and generally with evident interest heard my gospel messages. Through the kindness of the Cincinnati Branch of the U. S. Sanitary Commission, I was favored with a free passage on the Sanitary steamer ' Dunleith,' from Cincinnati to Young's Point, Louisiana, and started with an abundant supply of stores, so that I might efficiently minister to the temporal, as well as the spiritual wants of our brave defenders, on duty in forts, camps, and on our gunboats, from Cairo, Illinois, to Vicksburg, Mississippi. During this trip I distributed a large amount of reading matter, preached some thirty times, and conversed with hundreds of our soldiers and sailors.

"On a gunboat below Cairo, an officer wel-

comed my visit most cordially, saying, 'You
are the first minister that has stood on our deck
with reading matter for our crew and words of
cheer for us all.' On another, a fine-looking
youth, neat and trim in his blue jacket, met me
at the gangway with an earnest salutation, adding, 'You used to address our Sabbath-school
at home. I am glad to see you.' He aided me
to find my way over the vessel while distributing books, and kindly introduced me to many
of his companions. In the camps around Memphis, and the hospitals in the city, I found
abundant opportunities of usefulness. At that
time the work was great and the laborers few.
Now the Christian Commission has a strong
foothold, and a bright record of extended labor
and abundant usefulness.

"Descending the Mississippi, on the deserted
cotton-fields of Louisiana, in long lines of en-
campments among the heroes that captured
Vicksburg, with my fellow-laborers, Burnell of
Wisconsin, and Reynolds of Illinois, I labored
in word and deed with much encouragement.
On the floating hospital, moored near Milliken's
Bend, Louisiana, with its seven hundred and
sixty sick and languishing patients, I found

many hands to receive our gifts, and many ears open to hear the glorious gospel of the Son of God.   One poor fellow, near the portals of death, when I asked him how he was, exclaimed, with a genial smile and a holy ecstasy,

'In Christ I am happy day and night. All is well.'

"In a few days, as we were bearing him on our boat towards his northern home, he died in great peace; and now the mortal remains of Albert Conningham rest with his kindred in a beautiful graveyard in Central Ohio.

"At the Van Buren Convalescent Hospital, a few miles below, occupying a planter's residence, and the lovely lawn surrounding it, where the pride of China and the magnolia were blooming, and the mocking-bird nestled, we found eighteen hundred men glad to see 'somebody from home,' anxious to receive 'something to read,' and ready to hear our words of encouragement and Christian instruction.   In what was once a 'negro quarter' we found a band of pious soldiers holding a prayer meeting.   Seeing the grace of God in these 'bluecoat' brethren, I was truly glad, and exhorted them all that with purpose of heart they should cleave unto the Lord.'

"Another 'quarter' was occupied by colored people. I entered and said to them, 'I only wished to see "the slave quarters." An intelligent looking man said, ' Lor, massa, dis is not a slave quarter anymo, we be all free, bless de Lord.' The treason of their masters removed their chains, and gave them freedom. Quite a number of freed men gathered around me, and on the sill of the door I preached unto them Jesus and the Resurrection; and on the sod in front we knelt in prayer with these sable sons of Ethiopia, commending them to the God of all grace and consolation,

"Immediately after the battle of Chickamauga, with thirteen other delegates, I left Cincinnati for the scenes of carnage and of suffering. Travelling four hundred and sixty miles, I reached Stevenson, Alabama, on the 25th of September. Here I met Brothers Parson and Harvey supplying a train of wounded soldiers with bread and coffee. At once I was welcomed as a helper in this important work of relief. The poor fellows had made their way, as best they could, from Chattanooga to Bridgeport, thence by the cars thirteen miles to this place. Exhausted and hungry, faint and weary, they needed refreshments. Some two thousand loaves of excellent bread, and a bountiful supply of coffee, hot and good, these wounded men—passing through Stevenson—received from the hands of the delegates of the Christian Commission, the supplies being furnished by the Government, In our chapel, we held religious services twice a day, generally very well attended. Several of the soldiers became deeply convicted of sin, and earnestly inquired what they must do to be saved. Blessed privilege, even amid the fearful realities of war, to point them to the 'Lamb of God, that taketh away the sin of the World.' In our chapel I have seen from thirty to fifty soldiers attentively reading, or diligent in writing to their friends at home. In the field hospitals, near Stevenson, we found two thousand sick and wounded men. Here we distributed sanitary stores, which were much needed, and gratefully received. From tent to tent we visited the uncomplaining sufferers, doing good, as God enabled us, to their souls and to their bodies.

"The large quantity of stationery which we

distributed met a very pressing want, and enabled hundreds to write to their anxious relatives
and friends at home. While preaching a funeral
sermon in one of our hospitals, I observed one
of my hearers—who was lying on a pallet of
straw, evidently drawing near to death—very
much interested. Failing to repress his emotions, bringing his attenuated hands together,
he exclaimed, ' Glory to God for the hope of salvation through Jesus Christ.' At the close of
our service I approached the poor sufferer and
asked him if he loved Jesus Christ. With a
heavenly sweetness of voice, and a full heart,
he replied, ' Oh yes, and Jesus loves me.' To
this dying soldier, death had no sting, the grave
no gloom—all was bright beyond. Alas! All
our brave men are not the friends of Christ.

" Multitudes are hardened in sin, reckless and
indifferent to the claims of God and eternity.
In the tent, the camp, the hospital, we must
meet with abounding iniquity and irreligion.
Too many of our brave men neglect the great
salvation, yet we always found them accessible,
easily impressed by kindly words and good
deeds. The prudent, earnest, faithful, Christ-
like delegate, and the laborious chaplain may

go among them 'bearing precious seed, and shall return with rejoicing, bringing their sheaves with them.' God bless the U. S. Christian Commission.

"Rev. B. W. Chidlaw,

"Cincinnati, Jan. 1st, 1864."

CHAPTER X.

———

THE third anniversary of the U. S. Christian Commission was celebrated at the Academy of Music, Philadelphia, on Tuesday evening, January 31st, 1864. The building was crowded with an enthusiastic audience.

Rev. Mr. Chidlaw's address upon this inspiring occasion was worthy of the man and of the hour. He said:

' More than forty years ago, when a child, the speaker stood with his father on the side of a lofty mountain, near their home in the Principality of Wales.

"His father held his handkerchief to the breeze and said, 'That's a fair wind to take people to America.' The boy asked what America was. His father replied, that it was a great country, far off beyond the ocean, where the people had a good government, where poor boys could go to school and get an education; and where they had plenty of apples. The last idea the speaker

fully comprehended at the time, and he inquired
why his father did not take them there to live.
' By and by, my boy,' he replied, 'when the
Lord opens the door, we will go,' In a year the
door was opened for their emigration, and now
for forty-five years the speaker had enjoyed the
advantages of a great country and a good government, of free schools and free institutions,
and when armed treason assailed the life of such
a nation, and threatened the integrity of such a
government, he felt that, with the great hosts
of the Western boys hastening to the rescue, the
Welsh boy, who had here shared so largely in
the blessings afforded to the poor and the op-
pressed of all climes, must go and take a hand
in the fight, too." (Applause.) " But he had
always had a natural difficulty when a boy in
the woods of Ohio. He could never shoot because he had to close his eyes when he took aim.
While, therefore, he could not shoulder the
musket, or the rifle, he could cheer the boys on
and pray for them. The brave boys of the
Thirty-ninth Ohio gave him a regular Presbyterian call from the rank and file to be their
preacher, the officers sanctioned it, and he found
himself in the army. He soon discovered that

the quartermaster could not supply the want of good reading. Then he remembered that for twenty years, while engaged as a Sunday school missionary under the auspices of the American Sunday School Union—that noble institution that honors Philadelphia by making its home there—he used to ask for books and they gave them to him; and he felt sure that they would still honor the requisition of their old missionary, now a chaplain in his country's service. And they did so. He found, too, at the very start, that they needed something like the United States Christian Commission in the Army. They had groped in the darkness until, by and by, God called this great agency to be a light to them. He believed that the Christian Commission grew out of the great revival of 1857 and 1858. It was born of the spirit of prayer and union begotten by the union prayer meetings held in that favored hour, when those mighty waves of revival rolled over the land. The Commission sprang from a good source, and God had given it a most noble mission to perform. How well it had performed it, he had in many places seen and could testify.

The speaker then drew upon his experience.

On the battlefield of Perryville he had been privileged to go among the men and distribute stores. He found at Hospital No. 1, which was in a church, 2,400 brave men suffering from sickness and wounds. Instead of the pews filled with attentive hearers, were stretched before him rows of bleeding, dying men. He went to the first one on whom his eye lighted, and saw that he had had an arm amputated and was still lying in the soiled and clotted garments of the field. Most of the men were equally destitute. He commanded their attention, and bade them all cheer up, saying that their friends at home were near at hand to do them good. Having asked the men who needed clean garments, to signify it by raising the hand, or if they could not do this, by speaking, he then went from one to another with the shirts and drawers and socks, and all needed articles, giving to each the benefactions which were intended to reach him by the kind hearts at home which had provided them. When they had passed through one hospital in this way they went to another, and then to another, doing the same grateful work. One poor fellow, on being refreshed with clean raiment, said, "Preacher, I don't know who sent you here with these nice clean clothes unless the Lord." "Certainly, that's it, the good Lord and the women of Ohio. They were the partnership," was the reply.

One Hoosier boy, not over twenty years old, lay sick with a touch of fever and ague—an affliction which he had sometimes suffered from at home. I, comprehending the case, said to him, "What did mother do for you when you had these spells at home?" "Oh, she used to make me a good cup of tea, and such nice toast." "Why, that's just what my mother used to give me." "And don't it help you?" "Yes, almost always." "Why don't you get tea and toast here?" "Oh, the tea is not what mother used to give me, and the toast is not the same at all." Well, thought the speaker, you shall have some that is good, if it's to be had here. So going to brother Smith's ("There he is," turning to the Rev. E. P. Smith, who was on the platform, "and he is our Captain-General in the army of the Cumberland, and thousands of soldiers will rise up to call him blessed.") I soon found myself dipping into a chest of real genuine black tea, and a cask of loaf-sugar by its side, and a box of condensed milk. Then repairing to the

government bakery, I secured a nice loaf of
bread, and took it to the cooking establishment
in the rear, where the cook was. "The old
darkey—or"—(the speaker hastily correcting
himself) "the old colored man." (A burst of
merriment followed this correction) "Well," said
the speaker, half apologetically, "the people
understand it, and God bless them." (Resuming.) "As I said, I went into this establishment, and my dear colored friend, the old cook,
was there." (An explosion of laughter and applause hereupon occurred which for some moments convulsed the vast audience, and left a
lingering smile on many faces long after silence
was restored.) (Resuming.) "I began telling
him what I wanted, and asking him for the
privilege of his fire and utensils to do my work,
when he interrupted me with, 'In dis kitchen I
cooks and you talks,'" and he took the knife,
sliced the bread and toasted it, while we talked
of the blessed Jesus, and of his religion. The
tea and toast were at last made. The condensed milk was used instead of butter, and we
had a delicious looking article, which I carried
to the hospital.

"My friend," I said to the Indiana boy,

"wake up, I have something nice for you," "Why, preacher, ain't there milk in that tea?" "Certainly," "Why," he asked in astonishment, "does the Christian Commission keep cows down here?" "Better than that, my boy, they have gone all the way to the old cow at home, and it's all right. Now sit up, and eat and drink. And he did to his heart's content—indeed I am afraid he ate too much." A soldier close by said: "Chaplain, can you give me a little tea and toast too?" "And me too?" said another. "Me too?" "Certainly, certainly—we'll have a general tea party." And we did. The good old cook was notified, and he did the toast up brown, and the hot, smoking tea was delicious. We had a glorious tea party there. As a matter of course the preacher hung his banner on the outer wall, as an Ambassador of the Prince of Peace, and preached Christ to these men who had been so delightfully regaled with tea and toast that the friends of the soldier had sent to them. Oh, the glorious combination of humanity and Christianity. God has united them. We would not separate them. The glory we give to His name.

At another time I went into a deserted

tavern, used as a hospital. Seventeen noble
fellows lay on the floor. I ministered to them
in the gospel of clean clothes, and of something
good to eat. The next day I labored in the
gospel of Christ among them. One man said
that when he was a boy twelve years old, in a
Sunday-school in Stark County, Ohio, he had
been hopefully converted to God, but he had
never professed his faith in Christ; and that he
did not know that his comrades had ever sus-
pected that he was a Christian. He desired
now to come out on the Lord's side. I made
some remarks about his going home on a furlough—a returned Christian soldier—to testify
of Christ. But he said, "O Chaplain, I don't
want a furlough; as soon as I am able I want to
join the regiment and help the boys." These
are our soldiers! Faith has made heroes of
them. It is making heroes of our Sunday-school
boys, of our American youth in the army of the
Union. "Well, Joshua," I asked, addressing
the Ohio boy, "what church would you like to
join?" "The Church of Jesus Christ," he answered. As a recruiting officer of the Captain
of Salvation, I was ready to muster in this new
recruit. I talked to him about the articles of

war, tried to tell him what it was to be a faithful soldier—that he must not " break ranks " and
run to the enemy—and then, on the avowal of his
faith in Christ, I baptized this Christian soldier,
and welcomed him into the Church of our Lord
Jesus Christ. On leaving that cot, and passing out of the room, a poor fellow pulled my
coat, and said, " Chaplain, I am a deserter."
" O no, my friend, you have served your country too long, and have shed too much blood for
it (he had lost his left arm) to be a deserter."
" Yes I am," he persisted—" three years ago I
professed religion in Indiana, but I have deserted the standard. I have wandered from
God. Oh I feel like consecrating myself anew
to Him to-day—won't you muster me in, Chaplain?"

"This is the labor that is done for the soldiers,"
Rev. Mr. Chidlaw said in closing. " In this
way we strive to strengthen their faith, encourage their hope, and cheer their hearts. And the
work was full of reward to the Christian. To
point the dying soldier to Jesus, to hear his
pious ejaculations, to see the brightening eye,
and radiant face lit up with the glory of the
vision of heaven, to hear the rapturous exclama-

tions of those who are dying in the triumphs of
faith—Oh! These are ample rewards for all the
toil expended! And should not Christians provide the means abundantly for such a work?
Are not the men worthy? Are they not dying
for us? Shall we not open our hearts wide to
them? Shall we not take them in, and warm
them and love them? Shall we not only minister to them the bread which perisheth, but also
the bread of life for which they are hungering,
and which if they eat they shall never hunger
more?"

But perhaps the most notable oratorical effort
of Rev. Mr. Chidlaw's life was a speech delivered
on short notice, but with very telling effect, at
the great final gathering of the U. S. Christian
Commission, held in the Hall of the House of
Representatives, Washington, D. C., the evening of February 11, 1866.

A great crowd filled the hall, overflowing the
lobbies outside and turning thousands away in
a disappointed stream. The assembly was com-
posed of the distinguished and honored of the
land, representing perhaps more truly and fully
the powers which then wielded our great
nation than any similar assembly ever convened

in our country's history.   The Hon. Schuyler
Colfax, Speaker of the House, presided.
Lieut. General Grant sat immediately before
him, flanked by Generals and Admirals,.
Senators and Representatives, by Chief Justice
Chase, Bishop Janes, and Mr. Geo. H. Stuart,.
with other workers and speakers for the Com-
mission.

Precisely at seven o'clock the exercises began.
by the singing of the noble hymn of praise,

> " Jesus shall reign where'er the sun
>   Does his successive journeys run,
>   His kingdom stretch from shore to shore,
>   Till moons shall wax and wane no more,"

the audience rising and joining in the praise.
Prayer was offered by the Rev. Dr. Boynton,
Chaplain of the House, and a Scripture selection
read by the Rev. Dr. Taylor, Secretary of the
American Bible Society.

Speaker Colfax then made some introductory
remarks, and at the close said: "You have
already heard a minister of Christ who has acted
as a delegate of the Commission in the armies.
of the East; it would be proper now to listen to
the testimony of another divine who labored
with the armies of the West.   I have the pleas-

ure of introducing to you the Rev. B. W. Chidlaw, of Ohio."

(Address of Rev. B. W. Chidlaw.)

" Brethren:—When I was a boy in Ohio, my
mother taught me the lesson of obedience, and
I do not wish ever to prove recreant to her good
teachings.   Else, sir, I should not dare to stand
up before such an audience to-night, called out
so unexpectedly and suddenly.   But, brethren
and friends, I am ready always to lift up my
voice, feeble as it may be, for my God and my
country. (Applause.) The United States Christian and Sanitary Commissions are institutions
peculiar to the United States of America.   England had a Florence Nightingale, whose wo-
manly heart throbbed in earnest sympathy with
the suffering soldiers of the Crimea.   The
United States of America, embodying the great
principles of philanthropy, of patriotism, and of
religion, have embodied the sentiment and the
conviction, the piety, and the humanity of
Florence Nightingale in these and kindred glorious institutions that are alike the glory of our
country and the honor of our common Christianity.   The first delegate of the Christian Commission of whom I ever knew was a shepherd

boy in Israel. In the midst of war, when his brothers were in camp, his father called him to him and said ' My son, go to the front with this parched corn and cheese, and these barley loaves, and see how thy brethren fare, and cheer them with these presents.' Thus early was fixed the communication between the home and the camp. From this source—the blessed Book that has God for its author, truth for its matter, and eternal life for its aim—the Christian Commission drew its principles and its inspiration. And it has a history. We are writing it down to-night, and sealing it with these closing scenes. Its four years' record is complete. We are here to close up the army work of the American people in their homes, and, with the noble army that you had in the field, my illustrious General, (turning and addressing himself to General Grant) we have come to be mustered out of the service. (Applause.)

"The gallant 39th of Ohio was mustered in when the call of our imperilled country sounded through the land—a thousand strong, in July, of 1861 ; and with our arms and munitions, and our knapsacks strung, we marched for Missouri, whose soil the noble Lyon had just bap-

tized with his loyal blood. (Applause.) For
four years and more that gallant regiment made
its history. You had it my noble General (addressing Gen. Grant), in the midst of those illustrious regiments whom you mustered out at
Camp Dennison, in Ohio, last July. The old
Chaplain felt a glowing pride in his boys and
officers of the 39th, and went among them with
all his early love, to see them honorably yield
up the service they had been permitted to take
upon them for their country. Out of the full
thousand men who left their homes in Ohio,
only 309 were there to give up the arms which
they had so bravely wielded for the right, under your leadership, General, with such glorious success. (Applause.)

"Brethren of the Christian Commission, and
friends in this great assembly at the Capitol of
my country, we are here to be mustered out of
this service for our homes and churches, and
for Christ, among the boys in the field. Thank
God, the days for this service are over. But I
think now of the blessed work of preaching
Jesus among my men, of what good meetings
we had, what glorious prayer meetings, how
my Colonel, and the officers helped the old

Chaplain in his work, made his heart strong to preach Christ, and helped him in his efforts to lead the boys to a higher and a holier life, and to fight down the rebellion. And just such are the reminiscences of the Commission's work. But there are now no more favors to be granted by the Government; no more aid to receive at the hand of military officers. You gave your favors generously (addressing the distinguished civil and military officers around him), and we thank you, in the name of the people, and of the churches, and of all those to whom our work came with a blessing. You made our hearts strong and valiant to labor for Christ, and to do good to the bodies, as well as the soul, of every blue-coat man from the Atlantic to the Pacific. (Great applause.) We thank you, General (General Grant), and through you your officers; we thank the representatives of our Government, the army and navy, all, for the great encouragement and the unexpected and enlarged facilities you gave us in our humble ministry. And, my brother (approaching Mr. Stuart, the President of the Commission, and in the midst of great applause shaking him with warm earnestness by the

hand), my brother, we muster you out to-night.
We shall not meet with you again, nor with our
brethren of the Commission. In a hundred
places, and from thousands of platforms and
pulpits, we have plead the cause of the soldiers.
Oh! blessed be God, that He gave you, and all
the brethren who stood up for the Commission
at home, in behalf of the men in the front, and
reaching out to the great heart of the men and
women of the North, securing these six millions
of dollars' worth of blessings and comforts to
help the American soldier in his battle for the
Government, and for right and truth in the
world. (Applause.) Yes, brother delegates,
many a scene in the prayer meeting, around
the camp fire, in the hospital, in the tent, when
we talked of Jesus to the boys in blue, when we
mingled our prayers and our songs with them,
and bade them be strong in the Lord and in
the power of his might, comes to mind now.
Happy days! They are burned into these
hearts of ours, and we will speak of them when
the next mustering hour comes, at the last great
day, when the glorious Captain of our salvation
—Jesus Christ—shall say to us, 'Come up
higher,' and we shall cast our crowns at His

feet, and talk over His work in the hospital, in the field, in the camp and by the way, and be forever with one another, and the Lord.

" But, brethren, the reapers follow the sowers. We are mustered out to-night from sowing that we may go to reaping. Why, it is reaping time already! The other day, in a little log cabin in the upper valley of the Miami, I stood preaching the gospel to a group of children. A mother came up to me and said, ' Preacher, I want you to go home with me. My boy was buried near Atlanta. I want you to go home with me!' ' I will go,' I said. She took me with her. Reaching her home, she opened a little drawer and brought out a package which she unfolded carefully, and then handed me a letter. ' Don't you see the little dove in the corner ?' she said, 'and the words United States Christian Commission ?' What was it ? It was the last letter from her boy, written by a delegate of the Commission—her dear boy, her all. who had given himself for his country, and whom she had given cheerfully to the cause. Oh! how rich a country is ours, brethren, saved by the blood of such sons, of such mothers!—consecrated by the mother love of the thousands of bereft ones, who in the midst of their loneliness and tears, rejoice over a land redeemed, regenerated, disenthralled! Let us thank God, brethren, for our Government, and for anything we have done to sustain it in the hour of its peril! for our army and many victories. And Oh! whenever we see that banner, that beautiful emblem of our national life and power, let us thank God that it is unsullied and free, and let us, girding ourselves with His might, be nerved anew to work for Him, to do our whole duty, and to live for glory, honor and immortality, and all will be well." (Enthusiastic applause.)

"America" was sung at this point, with a positively thrilling emphasis. (Special dispatch to the *Cincinnati Enquirer.*)

(From a Washington paper to friends in Cincinnati.)

"WASHINGTON, D. C., Feb. 12, 1866.

"One of your citizens, Rev. B. W. Chidlaw, carried off the palm for eloquence last night at the final annual celebration of the United States Christian Commission. His speech took the house by storm, and thoroughly aroused the vast assemblage, who became perfectly enthusastic, and gave the Reverend gentleman round upon round of applause during the course of his remarks, and thrilled the vast audience with his eloquent illustrations of the noble work done by the western armies. His allusions to the closing labors of the Commission were so affecting as to melt the audience to tears. He was unanimously dubbed the orator—par excellence of the occasion."

J

CHAPTER XI.

RETURN TO PEACE OCCUPATIONS.

———

THE war over, the Union conserved, and the slaves liberated, Rev. Mr. Chidlaw, now better known by the title of "Doctor," returned to the quieter employments and more tranquil scenes of peaceful home life.

But this transition from warlike to peaceful scenes brought our hero no rest. He never knew how to rest. Some persons never learn that art,—till they rest forever, by the fine-ordered, frictionless activity of the life eternal. The termination of the war meant to Dr. Chidlaw a change of work, not its cessation; and accordingly we find him at once active again in all manner of lines of missionary, evangelistic and philanthropic labors.

Thus in 1866, in a manner almost playful, taking up the imagery made familiar to him by army experiences, he writes to that veteran Christian worker, Geo. H. Stuart, Esq., of the progress of certain revival efforts in which he had been engaged.

Camp Zion, Co. Ohio, March 7, 1866.

G. H. Stuart, Esq.:

My Dear Brother:—News from the battle-field will be acceptable to you. "Mustered out," we are yet in the service. I spent a few days at ——, eight miles from here, where the conflict was raging. Sixty slain of the Lord were taken from the field, crying for mercy. In the hospital, they found the Great Physician and the balm of Gilead, and were healed. Wonderful healing!

Among these was my own dear boy, now in Christ, and I hope that, with G. H. Stuart, Jr., he will yet stand on the walls of Zion preaching the everlasting Gospel to perishing sinners.

Four days ago I received marching orders for this post and reluctantly left the field of victory and rejoicing at ——. This post is held by a small garrison surrounded by an enemy 400 strong, and well entrenched. I found the garrison a small force living on half rations and with very little communication with the base of supplies.

Acting under the orders "ask and ye shall receive" we drew near to the Captain of the host, and we soon found that communications were

opened, supplies came and we have been skir-
mishing. The enemy will not come out of
their earthworks, only a few have met us on the
field.

We made a charge last night, and five of the
enemy cried for quarters, laid down their arms,
and are earnestly seeking reconciliation. Our
Captain is very gracious, and now three of
them are His willing subjects, and will take up
arms in his defence. Our supplies from the
base are increasing, the rank and file is growing valiant, and our orders are still " Forward."

We hope to meet the enemy in larger numbers to-day, and that our glorious leader will
plant our battery in range, and that the slain of
the Lord will be many.

The ranks are closing up, and we hope for a
decided victory.

Pray for me! My poor soul is greatly refreshed and strengthened. I never had more
real pleasure in performing my ministry. How
blessed are we when the Lord is with us, and
his arm revealed.

Your brother in Christ,

B. W. CHIDLAW.

Though a peaceful man, and not disposed to

quarrel with his brethren, he was yet a man of decided opinions, and of practical purposes, who knew how to lovingly, yet clearly, assert his opinions.

As a proof of his skill in reconciling differences, the following incident, which took place at a certain meeting of the general assembly, is mentioned: "During the devotional meeting this morning, which occupied about one hour preceding the assembly, the first half hour was chiefly spent by several members rehearsing the disruption of the church in 1837, their personal experience in the struggle, and other matters entirely foreign to the spirit of the hour. It was very evident that the large audience did not relish his method of conducting a prayer meeting. At an opportune moment, deliverance was obtained. Rev. B. W. Chidlaw stood up and read with emphasis from the Bible without comment: 'Brethren, I count not myself to have apprehended; but this one thing I do, forgetting those things which are behind, and reaching unto those things that are before, I press toward the mark for the prize of the high calling of God in Christ Jesus.'

"All felt the force of this, and like a nail in

a sure place, it had the desired effect. Windy speeches ceased, warm prayers were offered, with an occasional hymn, till the close of the hour."

All manner of enterprises commanded his attention and interest. One writes: "We saw Brother Chidlaw yesterday on his way to the Reform School. From thence he goes a couple of hundred miles to a Sunday-school Convention, where he remains until Friday, and lectures that evening; Friday night a two-hundred miles' ride to Cincinnati, where he breakfasts Saturday morning. Saturday forenoon, home, and takes dinner with his family. Saturday afternoon, to Aurora, Ind., where he preaches Sunday in the Presbyterian Church. Pretty good for the old veteran of sixty-five years of age."

Rev. Dr. Chidlaw's life-long love, the Sunday-school, never failed to enlist his sympathy and interest.

While in the army, he endeavored to carry out and apply its principles in garrison and camp; as long ago as Aug., 1861 (being then just on the point of departure for St. Louis), addressing a meeting held in the interests of Sabbath-school work, he spoke earnestly "of the great mission of the Sunday-school to afford personal religious instruction, with the view that those instructed shall be converted to God. This end, this absorbing idea, should never for one moment be lost sight of." The promises of God to encourage in the Word were quoted; the records of instances, many and sweet, of the favor and help of God were spoken of. The way in which our instructions should be imparted, always under the deep conviction that our scholars were sinners, unconverted, needing the new birth, was urged feelingly by the speaker.

This tireless and able advocacy of the spiritual claims of the children, inevitably had the effect of bringing Dr. Chidlaw into very prominent notice. He had become the apostle of the Sabbath-school movement, and his followers were from every quarter. The *Sunday School Times*, July, 1875, published his portrait, with this kindly notice: "Everybody who has ever known this veteran Sunday-school missionary will recognize the portrait on our first page. He is one of the pioneers in the work of the Sunday-school evangelization of

America. Earnest souls who in the earlier
years of a great movement throw their whole
energies into it, and devote their lives thereaf-
ter to its promotion, are the men who in the
hour of its triumphs it delights to honor. The
Sunday-school cause so looks to-day on the
missionaries Chidlaw and Paxson, McCullagh
and Corey, and Upson and others, whose lives
have been spent in organizing and cherishing
Sunday-schools during most of the last half
century.

"Among our American Sunday-school missionaries none has done a nobler work than
the subject of our sketch. Thoroughly imbued
with American ideas and with the spirit of
American institutions, which by his powerful
appeals and still more effective personal labors,
he has done so much, under God, to shape by
Bible teachings and influences, yet he is not a
native American. We owe to the little Principality of Wales the gift of a Chidlaw to America.

"From that time (1842) to the present, he
has never been out of the Sunday-school harness. Although during the war a Chaplain
and a Christian Commission worker, he never

yielded his Sunday-school mission, but in the army ministered to his Sabbath-school boys, formed his 'brotherhood' and Bible-classes, and Sunday-schools in camp, in hospital, and wherever he could gather the men to hear and to study the blessed Book.

"For the last ten years he has been Superintendent of Missions of the American Sunday-school Union in Ohio and Indiana."

In connection with this publication of his portrait, Mr. I. Newton Baker, editor of the *Sunday School Times*, wrote:

"MY DEAR BROTHER CHIDLAW:

"I have great pleasure in bringing out your portrait in this week's *Times*. I could have said much, very much more, but I forebore since you are yet a living, working man, and I am not yet called on, thank the good Father, to write your obituary.

"May our dear Father in Heaven, blessing, bless you, and keeping, keep you unto the end, and give you a crown of life sparkling with soul-jewels."

Everywhere he was cordially received. He seemed always in the mood for Sunday-school Conventions, and they for him. His was a

soul-stirring style of oratory. Someone who
was present at a Convention held once in Mich-
igan, thus recorded his impressions on the gathering:

"The afternoon children's meeting was grand
—the gathering splendid, the audience, music,
speaking, all that could be desired. Ralph
Wells—the last speaker—touching, thrilling,
good: Chidlaw, good, good.   *   *   *
The evening came—hall packed, gallery, ante-
rooms and all full.   *   * . *   Here Chidlaw made one of his greatest efforts. He carried everything before him. He spoke of the
army, and the kind of education needed to prepare the young for the battles of life. His ap-
appeal to parents was overwhelming."

CHAPTER XII.

LABORS FOR THE CHILDREN.

———

IN consequence of these successful labors directly with the young, there very naturally came to be applied to their eloquent friend the decidedly complimentary appellation of "The Children's Minister," with which title the *Cincinnati Times*, in 1876, headed a quotation from the *New York Mail and Express*, in which the latter paper had presented a sketch of Dr. Chidlaw's career, its subject being then in attendance upon the New School Assembly in New York:

"Rev. Dr. B. W. Chidlaw, of Harrison Junction, Ohio, has, perhaps, a larger and more populous church than any commissioner in the assembly. For over a quarter of a century he has been engaged, under the auspices of the American Sunday-school Union and kindred societies, in establishing Sunday-schools throughout the West, and during that extended period he has probably addressed more children than any other man in the country. In this field of usefulness his reputation is immense, and has won him the title of the ' Children's Minister,' by which he is universally known. But when roused to his work he speaks with great facility, fluency and perfect eloquence. He has the happy, though rare, gift of attracting the interest and holding the attention of children in the most remarkable manner, and his juvenile audiences never tire of hearing him,"

And then the *Cincinnati Times* adds, by way of comment on this sketch:

" Of no man in the community can it be said more justly, ' He goes about continually doing good,' than of Dr. Chidlaw. He gained the title of D. D. in the army. The good old Doctor protested frequently in our presence that he was not entitled to the honor, but the soldiers unanimously voted that he was.

" No man in the army was more venerated or loved than Dr. Chidlaw. Always happy and cheerful himself, he infused his spirit into the men, and made sunshine and happiness wherever he went. The great secret of his success with children is that he never grows old himself. He takes an interest in whatever interests children.

His appearance at the Boys' Reform School of Ohio, that he visits monthly as one of its Directors, is the signal for a general throwing up of hats and shouts of pleasure. The world is blessed in the lives of such men."

None the less hearty is this tribute to Dr. Chidlaw's worth, found in an account of a S. S. reunion and festival, published in the *Cincinnati Commercial* in June of 1876:

The eighth hymn, ' Over There,' was sung next, and then Mr. F—— said: ' Probably there is not another man in the West who has done as much for the Sunday-school as the man about to address you. You all know Brother Chidlaw.' Yes, they all know him, and recognize him, too, for he was kept standing for several seconds, silent, until the assembly poured out its ovation of applause. And then the veteran worker gave them a good talk. He was reminded on seeing them, of a remark he once heard by a distinguished statesman, that ' Children are the life-blood of the nation.'

" They had met with glad hearts and tuneful voices to celebrate Christian liberty. He told them of the Eddystone Lighthouse on the coast of England, placed there to give light and life.

And that is the mission of the Sunday-school—the light of God's truth, and the salvation of God through faith. The Sunday-school gives light through an open Bible, and it is a light-house kindled in more than six thousand localities throughout this land. The Sunday-school teachers are light-bearers both by precept and by example.

" He congratulated the workers present upon the success of the celebration, and encouraged them to further effort, in the language of an English nobleman, namely, that ' We must go lower and strike higher' for still greater and grander results in Christian civilization."

At a S. S. Convention held in May, 1876, at Hartsville, Ind., the Secretary stated in the Minutes the fact that Dr. Chidlaw preached a sermon to adults and children from the text, Ps. 34: 11, and added that he was ' too deeply interested to make an abstract of the sermon. The house was crowded and many were standing without. When Rev. Dr. Chidlaw took his seat he suggested that the children be permitted to withdraw before the convention proceeded to transact business; but instead of withdrawing, the children came crowding upon the platform and almost buried the old man beneath the flowers they showered upon him, thus fairly overwhelming their venerable friend and preceptor with this loving impression of their respect and gratitude. This unexpected scene, we read, produced a most happy impression on all the audience, and was a fitting close of a convocation of Christian workers."

"The old maxim, 'Catch the parent by first catching the child' is freshly illustrated by an incident which a correspondent of *The Sunday School Times* tells of our veteran worker, Chidlaw. Leaving the railroad, he walked five miles over the hills, crossing creeks on driftwood, to attend a Sunday-school Convention in Hancock County, during which he preached to a large assembly of youths, and three times the next Sunday. In the audience on the Sabbath was a gentleman of good repute, who had not been seen in a house of worship in twenty years.

"When inquired of, why he attended twice that day—did he know Dr. Chidlaw? 'No, sir,' he replied, 'but my children heard the stranger the other day, and when they came home they talked of nothing else but his sermon, and I felt that I would like to hear the man that could get such a hold of my children.'"

The kind of illustrative bait with which, in his happy, kindly fashion, Dr. Chidlaw caught the attention of his little hearers may be judged by one example, selected from an address delivered at Cincinnati, and reported in the *Presbyter*.

"The Rev. Dr. Chidlaw said that once when he was in New Bedford, Massachusetts, he heard of a whale ship that was just about to leave the harbor. Having never seen such a vessel, he went on board to see it. He found quite a number of boys and young men there. After looking round a little, examining the ship, he found the boys had disappeared. He asked the captain what became of them. He answered they had gone below to recite their lessons. 'What,' said he 'do you teach the boys?' 'Oh yes,' was the reply. 'we give the boys their lessons.' On obtaining leave, he went down in the hold to see them. He found them sitting round on boxes and chests, and an old weather-beaten sailor standing before them with a mariner's compass in hand, while each of the boys had a card with a picture of it drawn upon it.

Being informed that they were learning to ' box the compass,' he inquired what that meant. ' It is to learn the use of the compass in sailing upon the ocean,' was the reply. 'Well, chilren,' said Mr. Chidlaw, ' the Bible is your compass by which you are to steer your way as you sail through life. Study well that Bible, and follow its directions, just as the sailor follows the directions of his compass in sailing over a dark and stormy ocean. You, too, must learn to ' box the compass.' "

K

CHAPTER XIII.

VARIOUS TRAVELS AND LABORS.

———

IN a letter written from Philadelphia in 1876 he speaks of the observance of the Sabbath at the Centennial Exposition:

"The Sabbath, by the laws of God and the Commonwealth of Pennsylvania, by the firm resolves of the Board of Centennial Commissioners and the earnest approval of good citizens all over our broad land, is to be kept holy—the gates of the park are to be closed and a day of rest enjoyed. All of the foreign exhibitors except France approve the action of the Commissioners, and stand up for the American Christian Sabbath. Mr. Corliss, of Providence R. I., who built the great engine that moves fourteen acres of machinery, said that if the gates were thrown open on the Sabbath he would cover up his machine.

"At Paris and Vienna the English and American exhibitors cover up their goods on the Sabbath, while all other nations allow the day of hallowed rest to be desecrated.

"This Christian nation is not ready to give up the Sabbath or to jeopardize its civil and religious liberties by its abandonment. The struggle between the friends and the enemies on the Sabbath in front of the gates of the park, and the glorious victory won by the former, are hopeful signs as we enter upon the second century of our national life, and good fruits of the Centennial Exposition."

The impression his downright earnestness and undoubted sincerity made upon the secular press may be inferred from the subjoined account of one of the Moody and Sankey meetings held in Philadelphia in 1875:

"After the opening hymn, 'I Need Thee Every Hour,' prayer was offered by that well-known pioneer Sunday-school missionary, Rev. Dr. Chidlaw.

"His cry was for the descent of the Holy Ghost upon those gathered for worship, that all the Christians present might be brought up out of Egypt into the enjoyment of a loving Christian experience and a holier life, through Christ's dear name. The prayer was no formal utterance, but the supplication of a man who, during a long term of Christian service, amid hardship and difficulty and frequent discouragement, has learned to expect help from God in every time of need, and has learned from experience something of the power of prayer.

"On his return, in 1889, from a visit to England and Wales, Rev. Dr. Chidlaw continued with undiminished ardor in a variety of labors, most actively and usefully, although certain forms of work, involving more violent physical exertion, he had been obliged to give up—as he narrates in a letter to a religious weekly of the East:

"The *New York Observer* abounds in articles of special interest to the aged. Those published recently on the 'dead line' and 'crossing the line,' have awakened thought and brought comfort to an aged minister far down the declivity of life. He has been in the gospel ministry since 1835, when he was licensed by the Presbytery of Oxford, and since 1836 he has been a missionary of the American Sunday-School Union in Ohio and Indiana, spending several winters in the eastern cities in behalf of the Society.

"Though no longer able to ride on horseback, following section lines or blazed tracks through the forests, exploring destitute localities, organizing Union Sunday-schools, and preaching the blessed Gospel of the Son of God, he enjoys good health and heart to continue in his chosen work, aiding in the extension and improvements of Sunday-schools, participating in county and state conventions, preaching to the young in reformatories, pauper homes and juvenile congregations over his wide field. To-day he has no intimation from his kind and generous supporters—the Society sending him forth, or the Christian ministers and people with whom it is his privilege to co-operate—that his usefulness has ended; but, with courage, trust in God, and confidence in his work, he holds on at seventy-eight."

January 30, 1889, was a red-letter day among the business men of Cincinnati, Ohio, the occasion being the dedication of a new and magnificent building of the Chamber of Commerce. The dedicatory exercises were attended by two thousand of the prominent merchants, manufacturers, bankers, etc., of the city. The religious features of the services were striking and produced a marked impression.

The exercises were opened by the band's

playing selections of national airs. President Morrison then gave five raps with his gavel, and said:

"Gentlemen of the Chamber of Commerce and invited guests: You will please come to order. The time appointed for the dedication of this building has at length arrived. It is fitting and right that the first official act in this Chamber shall be a recognition of the Almighty God, the Giver of all good. We will therefore bow in reverence while the Rev. Dr. Chidlaw, whom I now introduce, invokes His blessing.

The venerable preacher, with a clear and distinct voice, and great fervency, invoked the Divine blessing upon the exercises and the enterprise.

There was an especial appropriateness in this selection of Rev. Dr. Chidlaw as the guide of the devotions of the assembly, for, as the oldest minister in the Miami Valley, he had seen Cincinnati expand from a mere frontier town to a magnificent city.

In the spring of 1889, Rev. Dr. Chidlaw made a trip to Washington, to which he alludes.

in a letter dated March 19, describing a visit to the White House:

"In company with Rev. J. W. Scott, D. D., (now ninety years old, remembered and honored by his students at Oxford, O., and Hanover, Ind., now scattered over our broad land, the beloved father of Mrs. Harrison, now the first lady in our country, and in every way worthy of the exalted position she holds), I entered its portals. With such an escort, and for old acquaintance's sake, the aged Sunday-school missionary was cordially received, and greatly enjoyed his call.

"Once before, when Mr. Pierce was President, daily family worship was maintained in the White House; now the worthy ruling elder, our Chief Magistrate, has erected the family altar, an example deserving imitation by all the Christian households in the nation. In the office of the Postmaster-General I was very kindly received by another Presbyterian elder, the founder and Superintendent of the Bethany Sunday-school in Philadelphia — Hon. John Wanamaker — genial and pleasant as ever, though overwhelmed with business and callers."

Rev. Dr. Chidlaw's war record, enlightened public spirit, and fairly national reputation, led President Harrison to appoint him a member of the Board of Visitors to West Point. His experiences at the Point are thus pleasantly described in a letter dated June 3d:

"The seat of the U. S. Military Academy is one of the most picturesque and lovely places in our broad land. God made it so. Its natural beauties, its historic fame, and its present use, render it peculiarly attractive and highly interesting.

"I was invited to preach in the morning at the Highland Falls Presbyterian Church, two miles away—Rev. (Mr.) McMurdy, pastor. The house of worship, a beautiful edifice, was built by Rev. E. P. Roe, once its pastor, as a memorial, and by him donated to the congregation. On the first Sunday in the month any cadets that wish may attend divine worship beyond the lines of the military reservation. Being communion Sabbath in this church, a goodly number of cadets were present, and eight of their number sat with us at the Lord's table, commemorating the love of their once crucified, but now exalted, Lord. After the service,

I had the pleasure of greeting these young men, and bidding them God speed in their religious lives. The cadet prayer meeting on Sunday evening in the Dialectic Hall, established by Bishop McIlvaine when he was Chaplain, over fifty years ago, is still sustained. The present Chaplain—Rev. W. M. Postlethwaite, of the Reformed Episcopal Church—invited me to attend this meeting, which invitation I gladly accepted. The hall was well filled, and three members of the Board of Visitors were present. A cadet led the meeting with great freedom and interest. He read the Scriptures with reverence, and used old hymns in praising God. Several oral prayers were offered, and, by request, Professor Pinkerton, of Iowa, and the writer made short addresses. At the close, these young men, dressed in their uniforms, gathered around us, greeting us cordially as brethren in the Lord.

"Considering the difficulties in the way, we are greatly pleased with the state of religion among the cadets."

CHAPTER XIV.

COMPOSITION OF THE "STORY"—LETTERS AND VISITS.

———

WE are now brought, by the course of our narrative, to the year 1890—the period of the writing of the Autobiography entitled "The Story of my Life." It was in November of 1889, that Rev. Dr. Chidlaw, under very solemn and tender circumstances, was called to make an address reminiscent of Old War Days. The occasion was the funeral (at Cincinnati) of General Edward F. Noyes, Colonel of the 39th Ohio, and ex-Governor of Ohio. It is recorded that in the cemetery "the old Chaplain," bearing his years sturdily, stood before the folded banner that once floated over bayonets with a look that told that his heart was in the casket before him, which contained all that was mortal of General Noyes. Yet with a firm voice he began his address by saying that he first met Edward F. Noyes in July, 1861, in Camp Dennison. Among these men were the 960 of the 39th Ohio. He remem-

bered when they were ordered to the front, how
he held a service on the field in the open
area, and thought his work with them was done.
But the next day he was called to headquar-
ters, where he found Col. Groesbeck, Lieutenant-Colonel Gilbert, Major Noyes and Dr. O. W.
Nixon. He was told that the regiment needed
a chaplain, and was asked if he would accept the
position. After due and prayerful deliberation,
for he was then over fifty years old, he accepted,
and he was glad to say that he never had regretted it. He spoke of the uniform courtesy
and kindness shown him by the officers, and especially by Major Noyes, and referred with
pride to the plan he had suggested to add a brief
religious service to the ceremony of dress parade. He had observed that it was received
with reverent respect by all the men, and he
felt that it was not unproductive of good. As
" the old chaplain " continued his remarks, endeavoring to give consolation to the bereaved
family by speaking of the promises of resurrection and of a coming re-union, his eyes ever
and anon rested lovingly on the flag-draped
casket, as if he would gladly call back to life its
honored occupant. He attempted no eulogy,

leaving that, as he said, to the statesmen and comrades of the bar and bench who were familiar with the dead soldier's career.

In June, 1891, the Centennial Ohio Sunday-school Convention was held at Marietta, an interesting report of which we append:

"The first school in the State having been organized in the United States stockade at Marietta in 1791, the Ohio convention this year celebrated that event by turning the third day of its annual convocation into a historical review for the five States of the old Northwest Territory. Foremost among the speakers for Ohio was the veteran superintendent and missionary of the American Sunday-school Union, Rev. B. W. Chidlaw, D. D.

"Although lacking but one month of eighty full years, he spoke with his usual force and fluency, and gave a very interesting statement of the progress of this department of Gospel service,

"The large assembly listened with deep sympathy and veneration. At the close of Rev. Dr. Chidlaw's remarks, Mr. Timothy Nicholson, of Richmond, Ind., said, 'As a Hoosier, I wish to say to this convention, let us rise up in the presence of this old man. Stand up and honor the aged!' As by one common impulse, at this suggestion, the entire assembly rose to its feet. Dr. Chidlaw was deeply moved, and all felt it to be a touching tribute to a venerable servant of Christ, and friend of the children."

That the veteran Chaplain's love for his country never failed nor even weakened with the advancing years, is attested by his ardent remarks on Memorial Day, 1891, at Athens, Ohio.

Although eighty years old, he said, the blood in his veins tingled with patriotism as vigorously as ever, and should the country again need his service as it did thirty years before, it would be as freely offered.

A local paper thus alluded to the enthusiasm with which he participated in the Grand Army re-union at Detroit, in August:

"Rev. Dr. Chidlaw, in his eighty-first year, late Chaplain of the 39th O. V. I., a member of Geo. H. Thomas post, of the G. A. R., leaves on Monday for the great National Encampment at Detroit, Mich., where he hopes to greet once more his comrades, and to enjoy the parade of the brave heroes who won the victories that saved the Union and the life of the nation."

"The Rev. Dr. Chidlaw returned this morning from Detroit, where he was in attendance on the National Encampment, G. A. R. The reverend gentleman went through the war as Chaplain of the Thirty-ninth Ohio, and, with flag in hand, he marched with his old boys through the entire route, bearing his eighty years lightly, for his heart beat high with pride and he felt as young as when he led the hosts of the Lord to fight in the forward ranks of the nation's defenders. He says Ohio did herself proud with her 13,000 men in line; and not an intoxicated man was seen in the parade. On the train coming home, a soldier from 'Dayton Home' was fighting over again a furious battle with his comrades, when the grim reaper suddenly joined the circle, and carried off the aged orator to his reward beyond the skies. Dr. Chidlaw says the scene was affecting in the extreme, and produced a profound sensation."

His old love for the soldiers and devotion to their interests continued through life, as will be seen from the following, dated

"FORTRESS MONROE, VA., Sept. 28, 1891.

"This celebrated fortification is in a locality identified with historical affairs relating to colonial times, the war of the Revolution, and the Rebellion of 1861. But Fortress Monroe of to-day only dates back to 1831, when the United States Government, at an immense cost, built these massive walls, parapets and casemates, offices, dwellings, store-houses and barracks for enlisted men. The ground enclosed by these strong defenses is extensive and well improved; venerable live-oaks, plants and flowers beautify the walks and gratify the eye. * * * At present only six companies of soldiers 'hold the fort.' At dress parade they made a fine show, and elicited the admiration of a crowd of spectators. In one line of casemates soldiers that have families live. These are chambers of solid masonry covered with parapets, an elevation of earth designed for the protection of troops when assailed by enemies. These rooms are fairly well ventilated and lighted, and make comfortable homes.

"At the end of the line we found the rooms occupied by the Y. M. C. A. of Fortress Monroe. Two casemates are used and neatly furnished; one is the reading-room and library, well supplied with religious reading, papers and books; the other is the chapel, where religious services are held on Sunday and week evenings. Eighty enlisted men are now on its rolls, and many of them deeply interested in its services. The Bible class on Sunday afternoon is well attended, and helpful in acquiring Bible knowledge.

"In the hotel I saw a notice of Sunday preaching in the Post chapel by the Chaplain. With several friends, hearing the church call from the bugle, we made our way to the 'Church of the Centurion,' a small frame building with Gothic windows of stained glass. Facing the chancel, aided by the 'dim, religious light,' my eyes rested on a stained glass window on which was the picture of what I thought, at first sight, was an aboriginal of Virginia, an ancestor of Pocahontas; but, on closer examination, and seeing a spear in the right hand, and a sword in the left, I understood that I was facing a Roman captain, the devout centurion. The Post chaplain officiated strictly after the Episcopal order. The congregation heartily responded. The singing was inspiring and the sermon instructive."

In the spring of 1892, Dr. Chidlaw, in company with his wife, made one of his ever welcome visits to the Western Female Seminary at

Oxford, Ohio, of which the following newspaper account has been preserved:

"Last week we promised to give our readers an account of Dr. Chidlaw's visit to the Seminary. It was a rash promise, if by it was meant that we could give any real or vivid conception of the joy and inspiration we received. That would be impossible. Such joys must be participated in to be understood, but all who know Dr. Chidlaw will agree with us that to have his cheery presence in a household could not fail to be a benediction to that home, and Mrs. Chidlaw's sweet, refined face besides his, and her hearty interest in our work, enhanced the pleasure of the three days' visit. Dr. and Mrs. Chidlaw came to us on Thursday evening.

"On Saturday evening a short, solemn and most impressive service was held preparatory to the celebration of the Lord's Supper. Mr. Waldo B.—— and Mr. S. W. X——, elders in the Oxford Presbyterian Church, were with us on Sabbath morning for the observance of this memorial service.

"We cannot give a synopsis of Dr. Chidlaw's sermon. It was no studied discourse. In earnest, tender words he pictured for us that 'Upper

L

Room,' so dear in thought to every one; he made us feel with renewed apprehension the significance and solemnity of that last supper of our Lord.

" When one thinks of the more than three-score years that Dr. Chidlaw has loved and told this 'old, old story,' and listens again to him, telling it with no abatement, but rather an increasing interest and belief in its reality; when one remembers how this belief has sweetened, and ennobled and beautified his own and so many other lives, one cannot but exclaim surely in this 'way appear steps unto heaven.'

" At the close of the solemn service, Dr. Chidlaw told us of how he came to Oxford many years ago to celebrate the Lord's Supper for the first time at the Seminary, and met, at Hamilton, Mr. Preserved Smith coming from Dayton and bringing with him the beautiful silver communion service which has been in use once or twice a year ever since, Dr Chidlaw officiating each time. No wonder that he looks upon us as his children, and that we think of him always as our dear and reverend father in Christ. May God spare him long to teach and bless us."

At the anniversary of the American Sunday

School Union which was celebrated in Washington, D. C., May 9, 1892, were present three noted men—Hon. William Strong, ex-Justice of the United States Supreme Court, Rev. John W. Scott, D.D., and Dr. Chidlaw. As was remarked at the time:

" It was an unusual sight to witness the presence and participation of three such aged servants of God advocating the claims of the early scriptural and religious education of our youth. Judge Strong is eighty-four, Dr. Scott ninety-three, and Dr. Chidlaw eighty. Wonderfully preserved from the infirmities of age, the trio enjoy life and its labors. Steadfast in the faith, rejoicing in the promises and hopes of the Gospel, they cheerfully await the will of God concerning them.

" In 1833, Dr. Scott, then Professor of Chemistry and Natural Science in Miami University, Oxford, O., signed the diploma of Dr. Chidlaw. The meeting of the venerable professor and his student on the platform at a Sunday-school anniversary in the city of Washington, after the lapse of so many years, was very cordial and enjoyable. To-day the officers and the missionaries of the American Sunday-school Union had a very pleasant interview with President Harrison at the Executive Mansion. This Christian ruler, the Chief Magistrate of sixty-five millions of people—a 'nation whose God is the Lord'—has a warm heart for every good word and work that honors God, and promotes the temporal welfare and spiritual interests of the nation."

In connection with the 33rd Annual Convention of the Ohio S. S. Association held at Lima, June 7, 1892, the newspaper notice chronicles Dr. Chidlaw's last visit to any S. S. Convention:

"The President in a few expressions about the venerable gentleman, introduced Rev. B. W. Chidlaw, D.D., of Cincinnati. Briefly scanning his busy life of Sunday-school work, he recalled that sixty-three years ago he saw the first Sunday-school in Ohio, organized in a log cabin, and fifry-thtee years ago God gave him the blessed privilege of seeing planted the first mission Sunday-schools in the State, the journey from place to place being done on horseback, and he then travelled through Allen and Van Wert counties. He felt the utmost joy in the prospects for the present, and supreme confidence in the Sunday-school work of the future.

" He quoted the first verse of the first chapter of Acts as reference, followed by an eloquent prayer. His address, directed to the pastors, teachers, leaders and delegates generally, was most inspiring. ' Ye are my witnesses, saith the Lord.'

"Sunday-school work was appointed and approved by God. The Bible had God for its author, salvation for its end, and truth for its matter. * * * Critics may hammer away, but the anvil, the Bible, will remain, the hammer will be shattered."

This interesting incident was also recorded:

" At the close of a children's meeting in a Presbyterian Church where Dr. Chidlaw had addressed the young people in his usual 'felicitous and instructive manner,'Thomas D. Watkins. an aged and esteemed citizen of Lima, made some remarks. He said that sixty years before, he had lived in Athens, O., and had attended the Presbyterian Sunday-school there, and that B. W. Chidlaw—then a student at the Ohio University—was his teacher. It was through his instructions and appeals that he first became interested in religion, and this afternoon he again saw and heard his teacher of so many

years ago. He was glad to say that to B. W.
Chidlaw he owed much of the instruction and
encouragement that had led him to enter the
Christian life in the days of his youth. The meeting of those aged servants of Christ and his
church, recalling incidents of those early Sunday
school days was affecting, impressive and
mutually enjoyed."

———

June 25, 1892, Dr. and Mrs. Chidlaw sailed
on the steamer *Aurania* to visit his childhood
home.

CHAPTER XV.

———

[To his son, Mr. John Chidlaw.]

LIVERPOOL, July 4th.

WE arrived safe 10 A. M., Sunday, the 3d, passed through the custom house, and reached this great hotel in a carriage at noon. We are in good health, and at 1:10 P. M. we go to Chester, twelve miles; will stay there one day sight-seeing. Wednesday, July 5th, we shall reach Bala, fifty miles, and stay there till the 15th. On the 14th I hope to celebrate my eighty-first birthday, near the spot where I was born. We had a very pleasant voyage—while the "City of Chicago" went on the rocks at Old Kinsale Head, on the Irish coast, and 800 people had a marvelous escape. We saw the steamer about a mile away, and several tugs helping her, so we did not stop.

I have seen but two United States flags up this morning. I pulled off my hat and silently hurrahed for my country and my home.

I went to the office of the Cunard Line this

morning (beautiful weather), and arranged for our return, September 3d. We have room 89, one of the best on the ship.

We intend to take things easy and enjoy ourselves, making the most of our opportunities, rest and recreation; and I think we shall succeed, God helping us.

Write to us often, and tell us all about harvest. God bless you all.

We shall be in Bala on the 14th of July, which is my eighty-first birthday, that we may devoutfully and thankfully raise our " Ebenezer," for hitherto the Lord has brought us."

Your ever dear FATHER.

Turning to his diary we find this short record: " After a pleasant voyage we reached Bala July 5th. Left Chester for Bala 2 P M.; arrived 4:40 P. M. This is my native place—born here July 14, 1811. Hitherto the Lord has brought us. Praise the Lord."

[Letter written while at Bala.]

"During our stay, the anniversary of the Welsh Presbyterian Church Theological Seminary was celebrated, an occasion of great interest, attended by a large audience from all parts of the Principality. Principal Edwards read a report

showing the prosperous condition of the institution and its prospects for the future. An hour,
with appropriate services, was devoted to the
welcome of Rev. Llewellyn J. Evans, D. D.,
Professor-elect.

"The addresses delivered, and the enthusiasm
pervading the congregation, indicated the im-
plicit confidence, the tender sympathy and the
deep interest of the Welsh Presbyterian Church
in our beloved and honored brother, late Professor in Lane Seminary."

*   *   *   *   *

On Thursday, July 7th, 1892, a very enthusiastic meeting was held in the Welsh Calvinistic
Chapel, Bala, in connection with the Theological College. Several considerations helped
to make the meeting one of special importance.
It was the close of the first year of the Rev. Dr.
T. Charles Edwards' Principalship, and his first
annual report was looked forward to with keen
interest. A minister of world-wide renown had
promised to address the students—Rev. Dr.
McLaren, of Manchester. The meeting was
also intended to be a welcome to Dr. Llewellyn
J. Evans, who had just left Lane Seminary to
fill the chair of Hebrew at Bala College. Dr.

Evans was too ill to attend, but it was hoped he would soon recover, and be able to give the students at Bala College the ripe fruit of his long years of study. The speakers at the meeting little knew as they spoke in glowing terms of Dr. Evans' scholarship and high attainments, and congratulated Principal Edwards on having secured such a colleague, how very near the end was. A large number of ministers had come together, for invitations had been freely sent, regardless of all denominational differences, and many had gladly availed themselves of Principal Edwards' kindness.

The chair was taken by J. R. Davis, Esq., of Treborth Hall, whose father, R. Davis, Esq., Lord Lieutenant of Anglesea, has acted for many years as Treasurer of the College, and has taken the deepest interest in its fortunes. The Principal's report having been read, and the prize-list also made known, the Chairman called on Rev. O. Jones, B. A., of Liverpool, to propose a resolution giving the warm welcome of the meeting to Dr. Llewellyn J. Evans on his advent among them. The speaker had been a fellow-student with him at Bala College many years before, and had formed a very high opinion of Dr. Evans' ability then, an opinion which was fully confirmed by the eminence he afterwards attained in the land of his adoption.

After the resolution had been seconded by Rev. J. J. Poynter, * * * Principal Edwards rose to introduce Rev. Dr. Chidlaw to the meeting. In doing so, he stated that Dr. Chidlaw was a native of Bala, having been born there upwards of eighty years before. He went to America when very young, and had there devoted himself to the work of establishing Sunday-schools in the settlements. He had established hundreds of Sunday-schools in various parts of the United States. If Rev. Dr. Chidlaw heard of a new settlement anywhere in the far West, he went there at once. Though he had been so long away from his native country, he had not forgotten his language. Dr. Chidlaw knew Dr. Evans well, and admired him as a Christian and as a preacher.

Rev. Dr. Chidlaw then arose to address the meeting. There had been much interest excited, and much speculation caused by the presence of his venerable figure on the platform. He was a stranger to all, or nearly all present; but those who heard his brief address will never forget it.

When Principal Edwards spoke of a man who had been born in Bala upwards of eighty years before, all expected to see some feeble, decrepid figure tottering forward to mumble out some inaudible remarks. But what was the surprise of all to see the lively, robust figure, full of the spring and elasticity of youth, which came forward in response to the Principal's invitation! Rev. Dr. Chidlaw spoke as energetically, with as clear and ringing a voice as many a man half a century his junior would have done.

If anything could have increased the interest with which the audience listened to the "old man eloquent," it was the fact that he spoke in Welsh, and in such good Welsh, in his native place.

He said he was one of the boys of Bala, born there eighty-one years before. It was seventy-one years since he had left the place, but he felt very homely (a Welsh expression meaning at home) there; homely, though he was 4,000 miles from home. He had sacred memories of the place, especially of the Green, where the great religious gatherings used to be held in his youth. He remembered Rev. John Elias of Anglesea, and John Jones of Llanfyllin, preaching on the Green. It was in Bala that he had learned to read his Bible, and he had continued to reverence the Bible ever since. He could also testify that it was by means of his Welsh Bible that he had kept his hold upon his his native tongue, when wandering through the States, and often without hearing a word of Welsh for a very long time. America was a wonderful place in many respects, and he could testify that it was a grand country to live one's religion in.

He had known Dr. Evans for a long time, they had been members of the same Presbytery for years. He had known him as student, pastor, and professor, and he had the profoundest respect for him as a scholar, teacher, and preacher. Dr. Evans had read and studied his Bible in the Greek and Latin languages, and not only this, he had not rested until he had become thoroughly acquainted with the language in which the Old Testament was written.

Dr. Chidlaw concluded by expressing the sense of loss felt in America at the depart-

ure of Dr. Evans, and his own earnest desire
and prayers, for his success in his new field of
labor.

Dr. Chidlaw's brief, but fervent address was
listened to with rapt attention by all.   He impressed everyone as being wonderfully hale and
buoyant, and like a man with many years of
life before him.   This caused the painful shock
to be all the greater, when in a few days, the
sad news came so unexpectedly that he had been
called to his rest.

Dr. Chidlaw with his wife left Bala, July 8th,
and went to Dolgelley to spend a few days with
Mrs. Jane Chidlaw Roberts, intending to return
to the former place on the 14th, in order to celebrate the 81st anniversary of his birth in his native town.

On July 10th he preached in the English
Presbyterian Chapel at 10 A. M., and at 2:30 P.
M., addressed the Sunday-school at the English
Congregational Church, and at 3:30 P. M., he
spoke before the Welsh Presbyterian Sunday-
school.   At 6 P. M., he addressed, in Welsh,
the congregation of the Welsh Presbyterian
Chapel on "Missions."

July 11th, 12th, and 13th he spent in visiting

friends and places of interest in Dolgelly. But in renewing the intimacies and remembrances of former days, he was not forgetful of his friends on the other side of the Atlantic. The last letter from his pen was written at this time, when, all unconsciously to himself, the sunset shadows were beginning to darken the aged pilgrim's path. Its hopeful tone makes it doubly pathetic now.

DOLGELLEY, WALES, July 12, 1892.

DEAR BROTHER P——:

In ordinary health and comfort, we have enjoyed the genial and satisfactory hospitality of Mrs. Jane C. Roberts, the widow of my cousin, John Chidlaw Roberts, since the 8th inst., when we came from a sojourn of three days at the White Lion Hotel in Bala, where we met Prof. Evans and his wife, beginning house-keeping in a very nice house. His health is improving; and we hope it will be fully restored. I was called to address a large audience convened to welcome Prof. Evans. The applause, by hand-clapping, cries of " Hear! Hear!" indicated the feelings of my listeners, and how the Professor was received.

"We have a delightful home, and every attention and kindness. In a day or two we shall go to
Barmouth, 13 miles by railroad, and look out for
a good place where we can enjoy rest and comfort on the sea-coast, and feel the inspiration of
ocean breeze and mountain air.   When we lo-
cate at Barmouth we will inform you.   If sat-
isfied we will rest there, till the last of August,
and be in good trim for the third of September,
when we shall (D. V.) embark on the " Aurania "
for home.   At Barmouth we intend to take the
world easy, and have the most comfort and rest
possible."   B. W. CHIDLAW.

But that was not to be! The comfort and
rest he was to find were of a more lasting nature
than any earth could afford. Already the command to 'come up higher' had been given to
the worthy soldier.   He had no idea, however,
that the end was so close at hand, though in his
diary on July 13th, there is this little note concerning his health: " I did not feel well—short-
ness of breathing and weakness in my knees.
At noon I felt better and more comfortable."
There is a record in his journal of an earlier
date (April 20. 1890,) which is strongly indica-

tive of the earnestness of the man. It runs as follows: "I hope God will keep me at work, bless me in it, and then take me home." The prayer was answered on the morning of July 14, 1892.

After morning worship he complained of slight pain and retired to his room, and in a few minutes he had passed from the Land of the Dying into the World of the Living. Telegrams announcing the death of Dr. Chidlaw were sent to the United States. The following letter from Mrs. Roberts to Mrs. Peck gives in detail the story of his last hours.

"BRYNTIRION, DOLGELLEY, WALES, July 14, 1892.

" I am sure that you were all very much shocked at the sad news which was wired to you this morning, of the sudden death of Dr. Chidlaw. He seemed in his usual health and spirits when he came down to breakfast, and made a hearty meal. After that we had morning prayers. Dr. Chidlaw read and prayed in a manner I thought I never heard him use before, so earnest and beautiful. In a short time the postman brought the *Cincinnati Gazette.* He took it up stairs to read the news to his wife, then he prepared to go down again. Suddenly a great difficulty of

M

breathing came on (which he had slightly experienced on the previous day). He lay down
but had to get up again, feeling suffocated. Mrs.
Chidlaw was very much alarmed at this and
called me. I found him sitting down looking
deathly pale and gasping for breath. We man-
aged to get him to lie down, and in about ten
minutes from the time he was taken he was
gone. Dr. Chidlaw has gone to rest from all
his labors. For him it was 'sudden death, sudden glory.'"

All that was mortal of Dr. Chidlaw was borne
with loving care westward across the Atlantic,
and eventually to Cleves, Ohio, his loved home
for so many years.

The funeral services at Cleves were most solemn and impressive—crowds testifying by their
presence and reverent demeanor of their regard
for the departed.

CHAPTER XVI.

MEMORIAL TRIBUTES.

FUNERAL OF DR. CHIDLAW.

THE remains reached the family home, a mile west of Cleves, on Wednesday, August 3, 1892, and the funeral services were held on the Friday following, at 2:30 P. M., in a grove near the house and church of Berea. Seats were prepared for a thousand persons and many were obliged to stand. Over two hundred came from the city, and about a thousand from other places. The services were conducted by Dr. J. G. Monfort, and a dozen others took part. Fourteen ministers were present, and many prominent laymen, long friends and intimates of the deceased His favorite hymns were sung: "Jesus, lover of my Soul," "Rock of Ages, cleft for me," and "Guide me, O thou great Jehovah." Prayer was offered by Rev. Dr. J. J. Francis.

Rev. Dr. James, of Springdale, referred to Dr. Chidlaw's work for the children, the hospitals, the prisons and the army.

A. E. Chamberlain, who was associated with

him in the management of the Cincinnati section of the Christian Commission during the
war, referred to him as the most efficient and
useful worker in the war.   .

Rev. Dr. Thompson, president of Miami University, of which he was a trustee, paid a glowing eulogy to his faithfulness, zeal and usefulness.

Dr. Jones and Rev. Mr. Griffiths, pastors of
the two Welsh churches of Cincinnati, spoke
with great affection and reverence for him as a
man and a minister, and with gratitude for his
frequent labors, for fifty years, in these churches
and their Sabbath-schools.

Dr. Monfort made the last address. His acquaintance with Dr. Chidlaw began in college
sixty years before, and has been very intimate
ever since. He indorsed all that had been said.
He knew no minister more widely known or
more highly appreciated, no man who had
spoken to more people in this land or abroad.

He never knew a man so determined and
persistent in his work all the time. He was a
lay preacher from his youth until his licensure,
and few men have written more in the religious
and secular press to promote the work in which

he labored. His death was appointed, and it was right. The Intercessor prayed to have him with him. His life was Christ, but his death is gain. He is made perfect in holiness; the companion of the spirits of the just made perfect, and the innumerable company of angels in the presence of Jesus, to go out no more.

The following extract is taken from the *Cincinnati Times-Star :*

" Last Decoration Day was a day of rejoicing for the family and friends of the Rev. B. W. Chidlaw, and under the grand oaks on the lawn of his beautiful country home at Cleves, there was a table spread. The occasion was a gathering to bid farewell to the good old grandsire, who was preparing to cross the seas to revisit the scenes of his early youth in Wales. He was the very life and centre of all the merriment, for he bore his eighty years lightly. The fond farewells were spoken, with wishes for a happy voyage and safe return.

" Yesterday, under the same trees, on the same lawn, the same family gathered about the same venerable grandsire. He had had a pleasant voyage to the land of his youth. He had retrodden the hills his childish feet had loved to wander over, and his hoary head had bathed in the sparkling waters of the crystal lake, where the sunny-haired boy had disported generations ago. He had returned to the bosom of his family, gathered again to bid him another farewell; and the boards on which the feast of that other farewell was spread, now upheld his coffin. A more fitting and beautiful spot could not have been chosen to witness the last rites of affection. A concourse, the most vast of any ever gathered in that neighborhood, was there to pay the last token of esteem to the dead. Everybody knew him, and from miles around the people gathered from early in the day till the last hour. The afternoon express on the Big Four road carried out a large party, and the officials of the road, in fond remembrance of their old friend, stopped the train near his suburban residence. Prominent among them were the comrades of the Thirty-ninth O. V. I., the regiment of which the dead preacher was chaplain during the war. These gray soldiers wore no uniform but a simple black badge inscribed in silver letters: "Thirty-ninth O. V. I." Delegates from George H. Thomas Post,

No. 13, G. A. R., also from the Jones Post, and other prominent mourners, were present.

"There was present a large number of preachers who had known the venerable deceased for decades. At the appointed hour a thousand persons had gathered under the oaks, where seats were arranged about the central tables. Immediately in front was the preacher's platform, to the right of this platform were seats for the family, and to the left an organ and choir. At 2.20 the corpse was carried from the house by the grandsons of the divine. The honorary pall-bearers were from the Thomas Post and Thirty-ninth regiment.

"The exercises were in charge of Rev. D. J. G. Monfort, the venerable editor of the *Herald and Presbyter*, who was a class-mate with Rev. Mr. Chidlaw at Miami University in 1833-4, and who was ordained at the same time with him by the same Presbytery. Dr. Monfort is eighty-two years of age and still vigorous, but at times his sturdy form trembled with emotion, and he could scarcely proceed with the services.

"Rev. J. J. Francis made the opening prayer, and after a hymn sung by the choir, Rev. W. E. Carson, of Harrison, a life-long friend of the deceased, advanced and delivered the eulogy. It was an eloquent effort, and had this peculiar quality that is lacking from most funeral orations—it was the truth. Every statement found ready corroboration by all who heard it, and none denied to the dead the many grand qualities of heart and mind recounted by the impassioned speaker. The orator was followed by other speakers in short addresses.

" Among those who thus made reminiscent remarks, were Dr. Thompson, President of Miami University, of which Rev. Dr. Chidlaw was for years a Director, and Rev. Drs. Griffith and Jones of the Welsh churches. After the regular services the body was committed to the care of the Thirty-ninth Regiment and the Thomas Post. The comrades gathered about the casket, and Frank Bruner, on behalf of the Thirty-ninth Regiment, made a feeling and eloquent address that awakened intense interest among the hearers. Then followed the impressive ritual of the G. A. R., led by Major Gane. The wreaths of ferns, roses and myrtle were laid upon the casket, and then all followed to the Berean Cemetery, where the body was laid and cemented in the solid rock. A peculiar fact is, that Rev. Dr Chidlaw owned this fine farm, and had built and maintained at his own expense a church and a graveyard for years, and he now rests in the ground he himself consecrated to the dead."

[Letter from Mr. John I. Covington, dated Liverpool, July 16, published in the *Herald and Presbyter*.]

" I can hardly tell you what emotion controlled me when I first read the notice of Rev. Dr. B. W. Chidlaw's death—whether it was gratitude for the many long years that had been granted him to bear the glad tidings that he did to those who needed them most, or sorrow that, while in the zenith of his usefulness, he should thus suddenly be called away.

" Rev. Dr. Chidlaw, for at least thirty years, had been to me an inspiration for Christian zeal and work. I recall that my father, who admired him as I learned to admire him, told me of his early life and privations, and of his faithful work, and gave to him the sincere tribute of his admiration for his Christian virtues and personal manliness.

" Twenty-five years ago I heard Rev. Dr. Chidlaw preach in Dr. J. P. E. Kumler's

church at Oxford. His theme was 'The Reform Farm Work.' His earnest manner, the
clearness of his exposition of the work, the mu-
sical persuasiveness of his voice, made an impression upon me that memory recalls at will.

"Since then I have heard him countless
times, and I have always felt, when he began
speaking, that the bugle call for a more earnest
Christian attack was sounding, and that the
enemy was immediately in front.

"He never seemed to grow old. He was in
the midst of the fray, ever ready to welcome
any help that came, but determined, if need
be, alone and single handed, to fight to the end.

"I saw him last at the Miami University
Commencement, June 16, at which time we
compared notes as to our then contemplated
trips abroad. He sailed shortly before I did,
but we hoped to meet on this side of the Atlantic, in his beloved Wales.

"Those who have heard him speak with infinite tenderness and love of his native land,
and have heard him, as one recalling the poems
of childhood, repeat verse after verse of the
Bible in the liquid tongue of his own people,
will feel that the faithful missionary has re-

ceived the consummation of his dearest hope, in sleeping his last sleep in the land of his fathers. Truly, a strong man resteth!"

[From a published letter from Miss Leila S. McKee, Principal of the Western Female Seminary, who was spending her vacation traveling in Wales at the time.]

"Rev. Dr. and Mrs. Chidlaw then proceeded to Bala, Wales, to be present at the Commencement of the Bala Theological College, and to visit Dr. and Mrs. Evans. On Commencement day he was invited to speak, seconding the resolutions of welcome to Dr. Evans as a member of the College Faculty. This he did in his characteristic fashion, rousing the audience to great enthusiasm by his stirring words. * * * Rev. Dr. Chidlaw spoke throughout in Welsh, with perfect ease and pure idiom, a remarkable fact when we remember that he left Wales when only ten years of age, and had lived in America seventy-one years. He attributed his ability to do this to the fact that his Welsh Bible had been his constant companion during his entire life in America.

"From Bala, Rev. Dr. and Mrs. Chidlaw went to Dolgelly to visit relatives. Dr. Chidlaw's health was perfect. He enjoyed meeting old friends and new, again seeing his relatives, and above all, preaching or speaking, as opportunity offered, a word on the theme of his life—the Gospel of the living Christ.

" On the Sabbath preceding his death, he attended three services. In the morning he preached a sermon to young people, from the text, John xii. 26: 'If any man serve me, let him follow me; and where I am, there shall also my servant be; if any man serve me, him will my Father honor.' In the evening, by special request. he again make a short address in connection with the usual missionary meeting. In response to the minister's request for a 'few words,' he answered that he was very tired, but if the congregation would sing for him a certain hymn which he mentioned, it would inspire him to speak as they desired. Much surprise was expressed at the hymn he selected, for it was one seldom sung except on funeral occasions. The words were Welsh, but a friend gave me a free translation, as follows:

' In the waves and mighty waters
No one will support my head,
But my Saviour, my Beloved,
Who was stricken in my stead:

In the cold and mortal river
He will hold my head above;
I shall through the waves go singing
For one look of Him I love!'

They sang this a second and third time—at Dr. Chidlaw's suggestion—with much earnestness, and then he spoke, as only Dr. Chidlaw could speak, simply, earnestly, eloquently, and appealed to all, and especially to the youth in his audience, to consecrate their lives to the living Christ, and to be willing in answer to any command to say, ' Here am I, send me.'

" He spoke of the work in America, for Home and Foreign Missions; of the hundreds of young men and women in the schools who were volunteering their services for this work, and mentioned especially our school for young women in Ohio (the Western Seminary at Oxford, which had been honored by sending out many representatives to fields in every part of the world. Those who were present said he spoke as though inspired.

" During the week that followed, his mind was full of thoughts of his approaching birthday (Thursday, July 14th), and he frequently expressed his great desire to spend it in his native place, Bala, with his life-time friend, Dr.

Evans. On Thursday morning, while speaking
to his wife of this desire, with his friend's name
upon his lips, suddenly and almost without pain
he expired.

"The physician who was hastily summoned,
said that there was no organic trouble, but that
the heart, weakened by old age and a long life
of unusual activity, suddenly failed and death
ensued.

"The news spread rapidly through the town
and was telegraphed to friends and relatives at
a distance, bringing to everyone surprise and
grief; for every one seemed to know and esteem
Dr. Chidlaw, though he had been so little in
Wales.

"Great sympathy was felt for Mrs. Chidlaw,
so suddenly bereaved, and nothing which could
possibly be done was left undone to help or to
comfort her. She was weakened from the effects of sickness on her voyage over, and ill-
fitted to endure the ordeal, but she has been
wonderfully sustained by the One who alone can
comfort in such hours of darkness.

*   *   *   *   *

"The sacred remains were sent to America
by the steamship Servia, sailing from Liver-

pool, Saturday, July 23rd. * * * * For his family and friends in America it has been doubly hard for him to die so far away. But it is a comfort to know that he was not in a strange land, but in the country of his birth—beautiful Wales, which he loved always. Nor was he among strangers, but in the house of a dear relative, a home rightly named ' Bryntirion,' Mt. Pleasant. From thence he was called 'to see the King in His beauty, in a land of purer light.' Ours is the loss; his, the infinite gain.

" As I sat in the little Welsh chapel, that quiet Sabbath morning, only a stone's throw from the spot where he was born just eighty-one years before, and heard the fervent prayers, the solemn hymns and the reading of the Scriptures he loved in the native Welsh tongue, I could but think of the ' new song ' he now sings, as he stands in the very presence of the King.

" Thank God for such lives as Dr. Chidlaw's! We shall miss him sorely, and the loss seems irreparable. During my past four year's service at Oxford, he has been a constant and welcome visitor, always bringing us helpful, sunshiny words of counsel from his rich store-house of experience.

"During his last visit he conducted our communion service. Those who were present can never forget his talk and his prayers. We felt as though we had been upon a high mount of privilege, and the experiences of that hour will never fade from our minds, nor lose their hold upon our hearts. All the communion services we have ever had at the Seminary have been conducted by Dr. Chidlaw, and thus he is linked with our Seminary life in an unusual sacredness. Following closely upon the death of Dr. Chidlaw is that of Dr. Evans in Bala.

*   *   *   *   *

"Of both these friends, veteran warriors in the cause of Christ, can the words of David's lament over Abner be used: 'Know ye not that there is a prince and a great man fallen this day in Israel.'"

*   *   *   *   *

The following is Rev. N. S. Dickey's article in the *Herald and Presbyter*, of Oct. 13. 1893:

"My first acquaintance with Dr. Chidlaw was in 1848, when I was a student at Lane Seminary. Drs. Lyman Beecher, C. E. Stowe and D. Howe Allen were the professors. They preached in turn every Sabbath morning. The Seminary church and students, and these Sabbath discourses were very highly prized. Dr. Allen, especially, was a favorite of many of the students. One Sabbath morning, when it was his hour to fill the pulpit, Dr. Chidlaw was in his place. Disappointment was manifest on the faces of many of the students as he walked up the aisle and ascended the pulpit. ' It's an outrage to put up every man that comes along to preach.' ' We are here to hear the professors, not these itinerants.' ' Are we to have another bore ? ' were some of the expressions of dissatisfaction which fell from the lips of students, as they sat together in the pews.

"Dr. Chidlaw preached a bright, pointed, eloquent Gospel sermon that moved and captivated all. ' If all who come along were like him, let them preach.' ' That was rich.' ' Good, good,' said the fault-finders of the beginning, at the close of the service.

" I remember another manifestation of his ability to control and interest men. It was at a camp-meeting a few miles northwest of Madison, Ind., in the summer of 1849, conducted by Rev. Mr. Vance, the earnest pastor of the Monroe church.

N

"On the Sabbath multitudes congregated, and continued arrivals somewhat interrupted the services of the morning. After dinner the congregation was called to listen to sermons, first by Rev. Josiah Wood, of Ill., to be followed by Dr. Chidlaw. A few hundred only, seated near the stand, heard Mr. Wood's good discourse. The masses of the people were standing around in groups, talking and laughing and running about, heeding neither the earnest, repeated invitations of Mr. Vance to come and hear, nor the tones of the speaker, laboring hard to interest and benefit. When the sermon closed, a short hymn was sung, and Dr. Chidlaw rose to speak. Such confusion as reigned over that ground, I had never seen at a Presbyterian camp-meeting, though I had attended many in early youth. The masses evidently had come for a good social time, and not to hear preaching. 'What is the use of trying to preach to such a crowd ? They don't want to hear.' The old Presbyterian preachers who used to believe in and hold camp-meetings were right in saying, 'They had outlived their usefulness, and had better be given up,' were some of the thoughts that ran through my mind as I sat looking on.

"In his stentorian voice, after standing and viewing the confusion for a minute, he called out so that he was heard above the noises and chatter: 'I have something to say to each of you. Tell that group of young men to listen; ask those walking about to stop a minute. I want them to hear.' In a very short time all were giving attention, when he said: 'I grew up in the woods, and helped my widowed mother to clear a farm, and have raised many a crop of corn. I always noticed—haven't you?—that the outside rows never amounted to much. The shade, if near the timber, prevents vigorous growth, and the stalks and ears, if they have any, are small, and these are devoured by raccoons and opossums. This is true of morals and religion. Those who stand on the outside, or in the outer rows, don't get much good, and never amount to much. Now, I am going to preach you a Gospel sermon, and I want you to get profit from it. Won't you come as near as you can, and don't stand on the outside row if you can help it.' This, in purport, was spoken with such good humor and earnest sympathy that it acted like a charm. There was such a rush for the seats, and when these were all filled,

the people pressed up as close as they could get
to the stand, the young men laughingly trying
to crowd in and not be in the outside row.

"When all had become comparatively still,
Dr. Chidlaw preached, with the Holy Spirit's
presence and power, a sermon which kept that
vast audience still to its close, and was blessed
to the edification, and, it is believed, to the salvation of many."

[From the "Herald and Presbyter."]

MEMORIES OF THE LATE DR. B. W. CHIDLAW.

"A small party of friends were spending an
evening together recently, and I was an interested listener when the conversation turned on
Dr. Chidlaw. He was my father's chaplain
during the war, a lifelong friend of my grand-
parents, who were from Wales, and one of the
ladies present had entertained him in Cincinnati.
My mother and uncle knew him well—so we all
felt him to have been our 'mutual friend.' My
father said Dr. Chidlaw was one of the very
few chaplains the soldiers would go to hear of
their own accord, and without special orders. In
Missouri at one time, during a particularly
dangerous period, when Dr. Chidlaw was to
preach, the 'boys' would stack their arms in

front of where services were to be held, leave a sufficient guard outside, and go in to hear their beloved Chaplain.

"After some time a horse was procured for him, but it was not long at a time, that Dr. Chidlaw was found mounted. He would come across some weary soldier almost ready to drop from fatigue, and down he would jump, saying, 'Here, do ride this horse for me until I get limbered up; I'm tired of the saddle.' Then off he would trudge, never waiting for any protest.

"Time and again he would do this, and many a soldier had reason to bless Dr. Chidlaw for his thoughtfulness. When he did ride he would carry all the muskets and knapsacks it was possible for him to hold on, thus lightening the burden of the 'boys' who tramped so many weary miles. His genial, loving spirit made the world brighter and better, and many a heart is heavy because he has gone from us."

E. H. GLOVER.

CHAPTER XVII.

LETTERS FROM PUBLIC MEN.

---

674 N. DELAWARE ST., INDIANAPOLIS, IND.

MRS. B. W. CHIDLAW:

MY DEAR MADAM:—Your late husband, the Rev. B. W. Chidlaw, was one of the very first preachers that I listened to; and, from the beginning, he attracted my admiration and interest.

He frequently preached at the Presbyterian Church at Cleves, of which my grand-mother was a member, and where my father's family attended; and his fervid eloquence made him a favorite with all who had the pleasure of hearing him.

His work in connection with the Sunday-schools of the United States, was a most extraordinary and useful one. Few men in the ministry had a wider acquaintance, or have left a deeper impress for good.

I heard of his death with very sincere regret, and beg to extend to you my deepest sympathy.

Very truly yours,

BENJAMIN HARRISON.

In connection with the foregoing letter, we insert one from the venerable Rev. Dr. J. W. Scott:

PRESIDENT'S COTTAGE,
CAPE MAY POINT, N. J., Sept. 5, 1892.

MRS. CHIDLAW:

MY DEAR MADAM:—Your letter, informing me of your great loss, but your excellent and highly esteemed husband's infinite and eternal gain, dated Liverpool, Eng., Aug. 5th, reached me in due time by mail. You informed me that you had sent his precious remains before you for interment in the land of his adoption, and field of his great and extensive labors in the sacred ministry, and other works of Christian benevolence—pre-eminently the Sabbath-school cause, to which he devoted specially the labor of his life; in which he gathered and organized more Sunday-schools, I presume I may say, than any other man on earth.

I need not say to you that tones of sadness would be inappropriate on such an occasion, but rather words of joy and rejoicing that the great and good Master has called to his faithful and laborious servant, " Come up higher!" and taken him to the reward of his labors—and that you

were moved and pleased to sweeten his closing
hours by your society, care and attention to his
comfort, during your short wedded life; and laid
him in the tomb, in the glorious hope of a better resurrection and re-union in that blessed
world where they neither marry nor are given
in marriage, but are as the angels in heaven,
even with the Lord.

I knew brother Chidlaw well, from his youth
to his old age—from the time he came to Oxford, somewhere about 1830, with his little package of clothes and books in a small bundle in
his hand, and a small purse of money in his
pocket, for his spare expenses in college, to
enter as a junior, graduating in 1832. I was
familiar with him in all his career in college;
and afterwards in his early ministry in his first
church in New London, a Welsh settlement and
congregation. Then I married him to his first
wife. He thence removed a short distance to
Berea, and preached during the remainder of
his pastoral life at Elizabethtown, near Cleves,
or North Bend, the residence of the old General
W. H. Harrison—with the family of whom he
was intimately associated in all his life in the
sacred ministry; and in his later Sabbath-school

agencies which were so extensive; and also his labors in the U. S. Christian Commission, along with George H. Stuart, the head of the Commission.

He was indefatigably laborious, and faithful beyond measure. I prize his memory among the most precious of all my pupils, and shall cherish it to the end.

Excuse any blunders or errors in this manuscript, as I am blind, having lost my second sight, and in the infirmity of old age, going on within a few months of 93 years. I am, dear madam, with highest respect,

Yours truly,

J. W. SCOTT.

[Letter from Ex-Governor Charles Anderson, to the Rev. Dr. J. G. Monfort, of the "*Herald and Presbyter:*"]

KUTTAWA, KY.

MY DEAR FRIEND:—Your reference in the last number of the *Herald and Presbyter* to your fifty-five full years of ministerial service, awakens in me, your contemporary, college mate and friend, such a crowd of olden memories and emotions, that I cannot restrain this expression of them. What an unusual period of service to the Master is herein disclosed! This thought must be striking to any considerate mind.

But your details of the membership of that "Presbytery of Oxford," at Venice, Butler Co., O., of the names of the men then and there present and active in it, and the solemn truth that, "of its thirty-one members," all, all are dead but two—John W. Scott and Wm. W. Robertson —startles me as would voices from the grave.

*   *   *   *   *

Of the brethren there assembled for presbyterial work, nine others were well-known to me. Seven of them were college mates, viz: John A. Meeks, B. W. Chidlaw, David K. McDonald, W. W. Robertson, Charles Sturdevant, Robert Irwin and Thomas E. Thomas. The first four of these were my college mates, (of 1833). And each and all of them were, (like Dr. Scott, but unequally and under far less severe trials than was that guardian and teacher), my unvarying personal friends, between whom and myself there was never one shock or jar to our mutual kind feeling. What strange facts and tender memories these must now be to me, one of their three survivors, you must imagine, for I can find no words to express them.

Nor will I occupy your space by any effort to portray and preserve herein the several characters of those lost and loved ones. Let their memories, my dear old friend, be silent in our two loving hearts, and in the hearts of any other yet living friends who may again read their names in these, our memorials of that scene.

But there were two of them, whose very distinguished lives and worth, certainly deserve from my pen something more than so summary a notice as their mere naming. One of these, Rev. Thomas E. Thomas, D. D., a son of a most able and learned Welsh minister of the Gospel and classical teacher, at Paddy's Run, in the neighborhood of Venice, was throughout his course at our *alma mater*—for above five years—one of the hardest students and deepest, clearest and most active minds, as was well understood by the few who well knew him. He became, in my poor opinion, one of the most exact, astute, varied and profound scholars in any profession.

The many kindly notices of that other common friend of ours, Benjamin W. Chidlaw, which have from time to time appeared in your paper, have often stirred within me a wish to speak out my little speech of funereal praise for my departed classmate and friend. But all of these tributes have been so peculiarly truthful, generous and complete in their commendations of his work, and in their characterizations of himself, that only a small margin of this duty is left for me. Wherefore, distinctly avowing that I fully approve and endorse every word of praise to his memory, of the many which you have generously printed and I have carefully read (and how affectionately eulogistic they all are), I proceed briefly to add the only unwritten word of praise which is left for me to write, and here it is:

Our class of 1833—up to that time by far the largest of the University—was generally esteemed by the Faculty and by the students (no mean judges), to be quite as distinguished for the ability of its members as for their superior numbers.

Chidlaw was a late comer into our ranks, an emigrant from Athens, in the fall of 1832, as I remember it. Of course, therefore, we had far less opportunity to observe and adjudge him than our older classmates, and in mere scholarship his grade was not high; but that is a small affair, since his inequality arose from a shorter, and perhaps a less good opportunity for studying, than the rest of us had enjoyed.

In his recitations and in his duties in our society (the Erodelphian), he seemed to me to show sufficient quickness and clearness of intellect, without distinguishing himself in either sphere. He was from the first, and always, and ever afterwards, the same kindly, cheerful, genial, all-loving heart, which has been ever since pulsing, all alive with these emotions, down to his last heart-beat, a few weeks ago, near his own native Welsh village.

There was never any change or surprise in the outgrowth of his moral nature. In it 'the boy was, truly and peculiarly, the father of the man.' But in the development of his mental powers, and their output in actual works, there was, or at least there seemed to me to have been, a very remarkable change or development. For if I had been asked, as we were sheepishly taking our sheepskins in the shade of the old College on that September day, in 1833, which one of many of the rivals would become our first in usefulness and distinction in the great world of which that ceremony was the commencement, Chidlaw's claim would never have come into my thought. Indeed, I think it quite likely that I and a large majority of the class would have ranked him decisively below the middle line.

And yet, what have these transpired fifty-nine years developed, or else disclosed? No one would now dare to claim for any other class-mate a competition with him, either in the sphere of public usefulness or distinction.

As for myself, I do believe that this poor immigrant, self-supporting, and mainly self-educated boy, has actually shown more and higher abilities, has done more and better public service, and therefore deserves more honors and praise, than have all our class added together! This has been my belief and utterance for these many years past.

For, with a fluent and taking oratory, and with a literary style of much clearness, force and taste—always with a "current" in and through it—he was, always and everywhere so diligent, energetic and self-sacrificing in the service of the Master, and of his race, that the sum of his public labors and of their blessings, is simply beyond any comparison with the like sum of any other classmate, or probably of us all together.

The long and active life of our dear friend, who helped you forward with his earliest prayers, and continued to sustain and aid you with his very latest labors, ought now to speak from his silent grave to you, to me, to all.

(From Henry A. Babbitt, Late Lieut. Col., 39th O. V. I.)

Pomfret, Conn., July 12, 1893.

Though I find in my possession few written records of the services of our devoted Chaplain, Dr. B. W. Chidlaw, of the 39th O. Reg't, and none of his later life, our residences having been widely separate since the war, I do find in my memory the strongest possible picture of his kindly, rugged face and sturdy figure, as well as his noble and heart-winning characteristics; and this image stands forth to all of us to-day, through many intervening years, as clear and well defined as though he had bidden us good-bye but yesterday. This is surely but extra evidence of the true greatness of the man.

It should be remembered, that the most competent and the best witnesses to the faithful service, and heroic devotion to duty, constantly shown by him, where those soldiers, whom shock of battle or swift or lingering disease had laid low, before Lee and Johnston had surrendered. Also, that those who, since that time, have passed into the beyond, and swelled their number to a great majority of the old regiment, can not now be called upon here, to pay their faithful tributes to his memory.

But all of those remaining will join in grateful remembrance of his wise and happy words of hope and cheer, his friendly counsel, his ever ready hand, and his winning, stout-hearted plead for each and every one who seemed to need an advocate.

We know it was his chosen and most glorious mission to *preserve* and *save*; and if this greater service to mankind should be the rightful measure of our homage, no monument or statue would be grand enough, no shoulder-strap suffice to hold the stars that would indicate his proper rank and place in our esteem.

No word of praise can add to the fame of Dr. Chidlaw in the minds of those who knew him best and longest. But in expressing the unchanging regard his comrades hold for his memory, we plainly follow his teaching and example, and thus may help those that are left to a stronger hold on all that is true, noble and helpful here.

I have also read his "Story" to members of my family and others, who had, in some degree, made Dr. Chidlaw's acquaintance, through incidents in his army life within my remembrance, and all have been much impressed with the wonderful courage, devotion and humanity shown throughout his most useful and instructive life. We see, both in his character and in his experiences as a pioneer, a notable resemblance to those of Abraham Lincoln, and we do, and certainly should cherish the memory of each of them for like reasons.

(From A. E. Chamberlain, Esq.)

CINCINNATI, July 20, 1892.

In all my intercourse with Rev. Dr. Chidlaw, running through nearly forty years, an impression formed that grew with the years, was his consecration to the service of his master— whose service seemed his great delight. To do good and lead souls to Christ, seemed the absorbing thought of his life. His zeal and earnestness had scarcely a limit. There was a charm in his simplicity and manner, that gave him

()

great power in impressing thoughts for good
upon the minds of all brought in contact with
him. To illustrate, I will give you an incident:
One Saturday evening, Dr. Chidlaw, Judge
Stone and myself were on board of a river
steamer, on our way to Louisville to spend the
Sabbath in Christian labor there, a large company on board, 200 to 300 passengers, gathered
in small groups entertaining each other. In
the cabin was quite a number of card tables in
use. About 7 P.M., Dr. Chidlaw remarked, (as
he looked down the cabin), " Brethren, why
may we not have religious services held in the
cabin ? I will see the captain and officers of
the boat, and report in a few minutes." On his
return to us he said, "We have their approval."
Having a supply of army hymn books and a
Bible in his satchel, he brought them out, and
stopping in the centre of the cabin, introduced
the matter in this way (without giving offense
to any): " My friends, in looking over this
company, I am impressed with the thought that
a little singing would add to the pleasure of the
evening. We have with us Judge Stone and
another friend from Cincinnati, who would talk
to us if desired." The cards by this time had

been gathered up, and tables moved out of the way. As the Doctor distributed his hymn books he remarked, " Now we want some one to lead our singing." Near the centre-table stood a tall, good-appearing Kentuckian, who seemed much interested. The doctor took him by the hand and said, "My friend, it seems to me that you could made yourself useful by your service." " Well," he replied, " I will do the best I can," (and he proved to be the right man). Dr. Chidlaw at once announced, " All hail the power of Jesus' name," and it was sung with a will. Our meeting was now fully started, and kept up with delightful interest two hours or more—not a person leaving the cabin until the close.

Nearly forty men and women witnessed for Christ, and no doubt great good was done in the name and for the cause of Christ. At the close, very strong expressions of thanks were given to the good brother for suggesting the services.

[From Rev. H. Thane Miller.]

Cincinnati, April 3, 1893.

I am in receipt of your favor, March 5, asking for some expression regarding impressions about my old and beloved friend B. W.

Chidlaw. I might as well attempt to give impressions of the lightning, or the earthquake, for his power was simply spiritual electricity applied to the hearts and consciences of the people; and his oratory was like an earthquake in its startling effect upon the audience he addressed. They felt the mighty power in their midst, shaking the foundations of their indifference, or their being at ease in Zion in regard to Sunday-school and other religious movements. I knew Mr. Chidlaw many years, always admired and loved him, and was proud to remember him among my friends. He had marvelous enthusiasm in his oratory, which was produced by his spirituality of heart, and his Welsh fire added to the love he had for the cause he advocated.

[From the Rev. E. P. Armstrong, Superintendent of the Training School for Sunday-school Workers and Pastors' Assistants, Springfield, Mass.]

My Dear Mrs. Chidlaw:

It has long been a wish of mine to secure a photograph of your late lamented husband, for mounting side by side with other prominent workers of the S. S. Union, who have stood with him through the thick of the fight in that line of work. Many of us, younger men, have for many years revered him for his faithful and successful labors, so wonderfully blessed of God, and as I annually teach the students of our school the work of the American S. S. Union, it will be a very great help to me, to put before them the face of one who has been so long a successful worker in this cause.

[From Prof. Charlton.

PLAINFIELD, IND., June 13. 1893.

To us who live in Indiana. Dr. Chidlaw's death was like the removal of a great landmark. His first visit to Vernon, Ind., in connection with the Sunday-school work gave rise to an incident. All ministers, colporteurs and others who visited Vernon, were in the habit of stopping at the hospitable home of the eminent Dr. B——. The first visit of Dr. Chidlaw occurred just at the close of a week of housecleaning, when Mrs. B—— was thoroughly exhausted. She looked down to the front gate, and saw a horseman ride up and alight, and hitch his horse and approach the house. "There comes another of those horrid colporteurs!" she said to herself. She went to the door, and there

met for the first time Dr. Chidlaw. He, as
only he knew how to do to perfection, soon
made them all feel glad that he had come. The
few days of his stay were especially joyful
to all.

Always after, when Mrs. B—— thought of
the many delightful visits from Dr. Chidlaw in
his missionary wook in that section, she would
express sorrow for those first cruel words, and
hope for forgiveness, closing to the effect that
we may "entertain angels unawares."

I knew Dr. Chidlaw as a worker among the
fallen. There was never a year but he would
visit the Indiana Reform School from one to
two times. It was his delight to be with the
boys. He was the best man I ever knew; and
here in Indiana, an entire generation are now
blessing the Lord for what Dr. Chidlaw did for
them.

[From Chaplain McCabe.]

CHICAGO, ILL., June 14, 1893.

I have been searching for an old scrap-book
I had, in which there was a speech delivered by
Brother Chidlaw, in the Hall of the House of
Representatives, in Washington, in the Spring
of 1864.

My only acquaintance with him was as I heard him in these meetings. I never met him in the army. He was in the West, I in the East. I remember him as a noble man, whose voice thrilled my heart. He stirred great audiences with his eloquent speeches. They were eloquent with fact and logic. He was too earnest for rhetorical flourishes.

There is no doubt but that Dr. Chidlaw was worthy to stand at the head of the whole corps of Chaplains in our great army.

He was the sort of man to transform a regiment of raw recruits into a regiment such as Cromwell would have hailed with delight, and would have attached to his invincible battalion of psalm-singing, praying, believing, fighting soldiers, who never knew defeat.

OBERLIN, O., July 18, 1893.

To THE MISSIONARIES OF THE CENTRAL DEPARTMENT, AMERICAN S. S. UNION:

DEAR BRETHREN:—Notices which you may have seen in the public press of the bereavement of our society, in the death of Rev. B. W. Chidlaw, D. D., are confirmed this morning by a communication from Rev. Edwin W. Rice, D. D., as follows:

" We were pained and surprised to receive notice of a cablegram from Wales on Thursday (14th,) conveying the sad intelligence of the death of dear old Dr. Chidlaw, near his birthplace on the morning of his birthday, (his 81st,).

" He was a grand, eloquent, godly man; the oldest missionary, and the longest in service that the American S. S. Union ever had. 'The shadows of earth,' he has changed ' for the sunlight of eternity.' "

Although some missionaries in this District, the Central, have but recently come into the service, and therefore are not very well acquainted with our deceased brother and father in Israel, yet several of us have long been associated with him, and all of us will feel personally bereaved. He was for many years superintendent of Ohio and Indiana. Brother Chidlaw's zeal, eloquence, good judgment and unabated activity, continued to a ripe old age, have made him conspicuous before the public as a man, a Christian, and a Sunday-school general superintendent and missionary. We shall greatly miss his voice in our assemblies, his judgment in our deliberations and his warm heart in our circles of Christian fellowship.

I shall be glad to receive from you, brethren, such expression as you may be prompted to make, in view of this divine visitation upon us. While we all rejoice that our venerable and beloved brother has been gratified in his wish " to die in the harness," yet we feel his departure, both personally and organically, as a sad bereavement.

Yours cordially,

CHAUNCEY N. POND, Supt.

CHAPTER XVIII

LATER TRIBUTES.

(From the *New York Evangelist*.)

DEATH OF THE REV. B. W. CHIDLAW, D.D.

By Rollin A. Sawyer, D.D.

A VETERAN in the Christian service, a pioneer in Sunday-school work, an evangelist of wonderful and abiding power, a specialist in charitable and reformatory institutions, a ready helper in every good cause for more than half a century, and in nearly all the States of the Union, his life was a blessing and his death is a sorrow. Fifty years ago he became known in the anniversary meetings of New York, and for many years the late Edward Jaffray sustained him in his missionary labors throughout the Central West. It is hardly beyond the truth to say that he organized more Sunday-schools, brought into life more churches, called more souls to the Christian life, sent more young men into the ministry, than any other man of his generation. This is a great record, one that will never be written out in this world. The harvests of his daily sowing "beside all waters," of his words spoken in the ear and from house to house, of his preaching in cabins to fifties and in groves to five thousand, have been gar- nered in many store houses; they shall be known only in "that day." His name is one "to con- jure with" in all the district which formed his jurisdiction as a missionary, with every by-way of which his tireless feet and his cheery voice had made close acquaintance, in the alms-houses, hospitals, and prisons, wherever his way or his work led him. You had but to name this man of God, this servant of man for Christ's sake, anywhere, to any one you might meet, to in- voke an instant response of interest, admiration, affection, to find a common ground with those who were strangers to you. To be able to say that you knew "The glorious Ohio Welshman," as a West Virginia stage driver once styled him, was to assure yourself of a welcome and some good degree of consideration.

What a messenger from home and heaven he was to the wounded and dying in the late war, to the sick and home-sick in the hospitals ! "Chidlaw," said Governor David Tod to me one day, "is a brigade of surgeons and nurses." It was a healing breeze to have him pass down the lines; it was his voice that turned the battle with many a poor fellow, just ready to give up the fight for life. Thousands of men remembered him as standing beside them at the crisis; old soldiers at the "Homes" tell of his ministry to them with irrepressible emotion. There has not been, it is not probable that there ever will be again, just such a "ministry at large" as his. The conditions are wanting; the man was singularly unique. We shall not see his like. To one who remembers Ohio in the "fifties," Chidlaw will always stand alongside of Jacob Little, in a niche peculiar and singularly separate. He was that style of rare man which you have no wish to merge in the crowd, or to speak of, save as a special theme. We mourn him now as nearly the last of that choice brotherhood to whom Ohio and the States adjacent owe such a lasting debt.

Near to the settlement in Central Ohio, made at the beginning of this century by the colony from Granville, Mass., is a picturesque region of rounded elevations of land, with deep depressions, a sort of sequestered rural paradise, very delightful to look upon, very restful and refreshing to a town-tired eye. Hither came the first Welshmen, ardent Christians, " strong for Christ and liberty." and here in the " Welsh Hills," Chidlaw's boyhood, from ten years of age onward, took shape and trend for the years to come. The struggle up and out into a trained ministry was such as to sift out all chaff. These pioneers came through the fire. Not by any high roads do men of greatest worth come into place to-day. But now tests are changed. Self discipline does not always come through bodily hardship, toil, and the hunger of poverty. Yet in that rude school, majestic spirits are fashioned for the times that could not afford a better. The snare of manhood to-day is self-indulgence. If a man flinch from that which is hard to bear or unpleasing to do, he sells his manhood and his birthright together. Upward through discouragement, opposition, conflict of claims on his time and his affections, the young Chidlaw slowly climbed to an education for the Christian ministry. So sublime is the "call" to which they march, whom Christ has chosen for a special work. It seemed sometimes a " voice " in the ear. The soul heard it always. Chidlaw at times spoke of his " call." Once, on the Ohio

River, he told, in a steamer's saloon, how he came to be a minister and a missionary. Men said: " It is one of the prophets risen again."

But you saw in the very " air" about him that alertness, that " wakeful waiting " of a ready spirit for the bugle call. This was the attitude of the man: he was ever poised for flight: he slumbered even on the wing, like the eagles. So strong, so enduring was that original impulse. There was no professionalism in his calling. He let no currents float him, he sought no eddies in which to drift. His way was original, as if each day's work was inspired. When asked his plans, " I have none," was his answer. " I go as the Lord, my God, shall call!" There was the same ineffable quality in his speech and preaching, that immediate touch and contact with the divine, the heavenly, " When he speaks, I seem to see God," said a child one day. It is the mystic power of a soul in communion with Jehovah, of a man baptized into the Messias. He had rare gifts as an orator— the Welsh fire, a voice full of sweetness and magnetic quality, a fervid fancy, and the soul of a bard. All this was a help to him. But yet the great charm of Chidlaw was something deeper and higher; it was the atmosphere of heaven which surrounds a godly man and suggests the halo over the head of a saint. He was a power anywhere—in a prayer-meeting, a conference, or an anniversary. When he took hold of an occasion, it was a helpful, masterful hand, never superfluous, never in the way, but always good and suggestive of the best and highest In the "open air meetings," once common in the West, under the magnificent trees of those primeval woods, Chidlaw was an inspiring speaker. It has been said that he had no peer for such occasions. But it was no shallow talking, no trick of oratory, no hysterical cry to excitable crowds; his was the strong, honest speech of a man who felt the truth and who knew the needs of men and the way into their heart's confidence and love. And in and through it all was that air of other-worldliness which made him matchless on occasion. "If he had suddenly been transfigured and soared up to heaven in our sight, it would have seemed fitting," is the expression of the sentiment of the audiences he uplifted in his rapt hours of "reasoning of righteousness, temperance, and judgment to come."

His death on his 81st birthday, and at his

birthplace, to which he had gone with his newly-married wife to visit, has only been reported by cable. There is something fitting and beautiful in it. He did not grow old. There was youth in his eye, his smile, his hand-clasp, his joyous good-bye as he sailed away only a few days ago. In his soaring up so soon to heaven from the hills of his native Wales, we see a fit close, a fortunate finish of the picture. If it seemed to cut short any plan of rest or of life in new conditions, to him there could be no call of God which could find him unready. We do not see the lower side of the scene, because he so constantly looked on the upper and the heavenly. The sun of his life does not set, it goes out into the glory of the life beyond.

[From the Cincinnati Gazette.]

REV. B. W. CHIDLAW, D. D.

By Murat Halstead, in the Commercial Gazette.

I have read with sympathetic interest the intelligence of the death, in his native land, Wales, and his burial in the soil he loved best, Ohio, of my near and dear friend, Rev. B. W. Chidlaw. It seems to me there is due from me, in memory of years long ago, a few words of him, for when I was very young he was good to me, and his inspiring teachings had a genial and profitable influence upon my life, that it has always been a pleasure to remember, and is now as ever a sincere enjoyment to acknowledge. After my first and best teacher at home, he it was who revealed to me the wonders that are in books, glimpses of the glories of the world of literature: and, with the exception of the venerable Dr. Scott, he was the last of the generation of men who were active in affairs during my boyhood, and gave me precious words of encouragement.

Mr. Chidlaw was the minister of the congregation in the neighborhood where I was born, and an excellent example of a gifted, ardent young pastor. He preached and prayed and sang in Welsh and English, and in his glowing energy was ever seeking good works, that he might enlarge his labors and his usefulness. He was the vivid living centre in the village and its surrounding farms. He was an orator, and there was a sparkle in his language, and a cadence in his declamation that arrested attention and commanded regard. He was personally attractive. A widow's son, he was so good and bright a boy that the ladies of his mother's

church required that he should be a minister, he had to go to Oxford College, in
Butler Co., Ohio, the same school from which
President Harrison and Whitelaw Reid gradu-
ated.

In his manhood and his ministry he justified
the judgment of the ladies who declared the
promise of his schoolboy days. He knew all
the little boys for miles around, and they could
not resist his sunny face and winning ways. He
was himself to them a big boy, and they were
charmed to find such a companion in one whose
pulpit thunderings were so impressive.

Some one told him I was a boy fond of books,
and reading Plutarch's Lives, Rollin's Ancient
History, the History of Greece and Rome, Jo-
sephus, and such works, at an age that it was
preposterous, for I should have stuck to prayer
and the spelling-book. Mr. Chidlaw soon had
his hand on my head, and majestically commu-
nicated the fascinating secret that he had a
big book-case filled with new editions of choice
works, all of the same size, and bound in linen.
It was delightful to know the case was never
locked, and I was expected to go straight to
his house whenever I pleased, say I wanted a

book, select it and carry it off. Mr. Chidlaw knew a boy well enough to not tell him to be careful with the book and sure to return it soon. I saw that I had suddenly become rich.

Among the volumes from the treasure-house were the Life of Alexander the Great, the Life of Charles XII., Charles II., the Life of Lord Nelson, and the History of Venice, and also, more surprising than all, the History of Athens.

In the winters, Mr. Chidlaw taught in his church a school which it was my privilege two winters to attend. It was very different from the common schools; that is, Mr. Chidlaw was there, and it was agreeable to be reasonably good where he was. He had a way of getting the best things out of pupils, who were his best beloved friends. Bad boys and girls were simply in that atmosphere impossible. Mr. Chidlaw revised my first compositions, and heard my first recitations. How well I remember the touch of his pencil, the tone of his admonition, above all his patience and his enthusiasm. I go back fifty years, and this time was years beyond that. Mr. Chidlaw was then under thirty years of age, and died the other day over eighty.

When our paths parted I must have been nearly thirteen, but I seldom passed a year without meeting him, and we had always something to tell each other. It may have been Mr. Chidlaw's influence that brought men of high reputation to our quiet valley, Dr. Lyman Beecher, Dr. Thornton Mills, Dr. Thomas E. Thomas, were among them.

Mr. Chidlaw was of slender figure, alert, elastic, his eye keen, his hair a mass of auburn rings that retained undisturbed, their golden gloss and curl more than forty years. He could not keep out of the war, and had to go as a chaplain. He was an ideal Chaplain, known to the whole army with which he served for his earnestness, his fearlessness, his friendliness, his affectionate devotion to the soldiers, his tender ministrations in times of trouble, his charities, his patriotism, the pathos of his services amidst the perils of warfare, his eloquence, that was quickening as a bugle note.

He was happy in his death—no tedious interval of weakness and pain before the end; happy too, in this, that the last scenes of earth for him were among the beautiful mountains upon which his eyes first opened. After eighty years of eager life given to the appointed work of the Master he worshiped, in the fullness of the faith that says and sings, "I know that my Redeemer liveth," he sleeps in honor and peace ever more.

[The following sketch of Dr. B. W. Chidlaw's army life, as Chaplain of the 39th O. V. I., 1861–62, is from the pen of Dr. O. W. Nixon, late Surgeon of the Army.]

I had known Dr. Chidlaw prior to the War of the Rebellion, as an eloquent minister, and as an earnest advocate for Sunday-schools, but I did not know him as a man in the best meaning of the term, until I marched and tented with him, and saw him tested as no other life tests a man. The office of Chaplain in the volunteer service of the Union Army, at the beginning of the war, was by no means a sinecure. A regiment, made up of 1,000 of even the best men, cut off from home restraints, and the many helpful influences which society throws around them, requires tact and wisdom on the part of the officers in command, if they are kept from retrograding.

I always considered that it was a great, good fortune for "The Groesbeck Regiment" (the

39th O. V. I.) that Dr. Chidlaw was chosen Chaplain. It is safe to assert that in the intelligence and patriotism of the rank and file, to say nothing of its field officers, who richly won their honors in the long contest, it was the peer of any regiment in the service.

Dr. Chidlaw was a good judge of men, and he entered upon his duties with all the enthusiasm of his nature. He did not begin by preaching or scolding over soldier's pranks, but he set about knowing his men personally, as well as by name. He visited them in their tents; he was an interested spectator often at their hard drills; he was present and encouraged all the manly sports that broke the tedium of army life, and he was as gentle and thoughtful as a woman when any one of them was sick. His tact often called for my admiration when I saw how complete was his influence, even over the wildest characters of the command.

At the opening months of the war, men were often sent to the field poorly equipped and with limited supplies, and it often required eloquent pleading and earnest efforts of officers to make them contented and amiable. There were vices also to be corrected, as well as discipline to be enforced. Prominent among the vices was gambling for money and profanity. I never heard Dr. Chidlaw publicly reprimand any soldier for such offences. I have seen him, when on his rounds of visit to the tents, come unexpectedly upon a company of gamblers, but he did not appear to see a card or aught that was wrong. It is doubtless true that he earnestly labored with many for such offences, but in such a way as to win them. Instead of fearing, they learned to love and honor the man. Before three months of service I doubt whether there was a soldier in the regiment that did not honor him as a minister, while they loved the comradeship and manhood of the man. They were at all times looking out for his comfort, and few there were that would not have shared the best of their rations, and given him half of their blanket. I recall a little incident which illustrates what I have tried to express. We were called to make a sudden forced march, and the horse that the Doctor had been using had been taken by the Quartermaster for a temporary purpose, and none other was to be had. But Chidlaw stepped out as lively as any of the boys of twenty-one, and said, " I

will go; I can march." All the officers were
willing, and insisted upon his occasionally taking a mount. I overheard the boys talking,
and they said in substance, " Here we are
among rebs ; we pay them two prices for
everything we get, and then they get behind
logs and shoot us. There are plenty of reb
horses, and here is the good old Doctor slush-
ing through reb mud on foot." The result of
it was, that at the first halt for an hour's rest,
a squad, I think from Co. D, disappeared, and
before the bugle sounded for the march, they
came up leading an old horse upon which was
a saddle much more ancient than the horse, and
his bridle was apparently a piece of clothes-
line. The Doctor mounted without asking
questions, and the boys thought it a capital
joke. A few hours after, one of the blooded
horses hitched to an ammunition wagon, balked.
He was unharnessed, and Chidlaw's bony Bu-
cephalus took his place, and he was again fixed
with a superb mount. Many years after the
war I twitted the Doctor jokingly on the time
he rode that ancient rebel horse impressed by
Co. D. I found that he had wisely judged the
entire affair. He did not choose to humiliate

the boys by refusing their kindness, but he quietly saw the Quartermaster, and was assured
that he would see to it that full value for the
animal would be paid. As Surgeon, I perhaps
came more constantly in contact with the Chaplain, and know better the excellence of his work
than any other man. He was a wise adviser to
the strong, and a tender nurse to the sick. He
brought into the sick tent and hospital joyous-
ness rather than a long face. His voice, his
face and his acts were always full of cheer; and
I never feared Chidlaw would depress and do
harm in the gravest cases.

No man born under the stars and stripes ever
honored and loved the flag, and the principles
it represents, more certainly, than did this son
by adoption. Besides, he had the talent to in-
fuse the same spirit by his eloquence in all
those about him. He was always brimming
over with patriotism; and from the day he entered the regiment, he began the educational
work which permeated every part of it. He
was a model of courtesy, and never trespassed
upon the rights of others. Side by side with
the 39th O. V. I., was the 27th Ohio, with another notably good Chaplain—the Rev. Dr.

Eaton, since Chief of the Freedmen's Bureau, now President of Marietta College. The regiments were scarcely separated during the war, and Dr. Chidlaw was almost as well known and loved by the boys of the 27th. But his active labor was mainly with his own men. It was a patient education in morals, in discipline and patriotism. His success was marked. A guard tent was a thing almost unknown, and seldom needed in the 39th. As for patriotism, when the three years were up, and a call was made for veteran re-enlistments, I believe the records bear me out in saying the 39th furnished a longer list of re-enlisted veterans than any other regiment of the Western army. I may here add, that as bullets and disease thinned the ranks, new re-enlistments were constantly added, and the rolls of the 39th have on it over 3,000 names. While due credit is given to the heroic and patriotic officers of the regiment (no regiment had grander men), yet Chidlaw is always to be classed among the early educators. The historian has never dwelt enough upon the wonderful education of the old Union army while in the field. I take the 39th Ohio as an example. When it entered the service, I believe it is safe to say

there were not more than twenty-five Abolitionists in it. Nothing would arouse the men quicker to resent it, than to suggest that they were fighting "to free the niggers." That they got bravely over this, history abundantly proves, while it also brings prominently to the front, that an American army has both soul and mind, and is capable of education while it carried a musket. The men at first looked on with apparent indifference, and even aided slave-owners to recapture their slaves, who from time to time found a temporary home in our camps. There came a time also when they did not. They started in as patriots to defend the flag—and justice and humanity soon joined hands in their patriotism. It was an educational growth, day by day, stimulated by events which no man directed. The men sang:

"Our father's God to thee,
Land of the noble free,
Of thee we sing;"

and would turn to see a black slave, tried and handcuffed, marching out of camp in front of his master.

With the surroundings before mentioned, those who have not had the experience can yet

scarcely understand their transforming and ed-
ucating power. In a weary forced march at
night, when there was no reason for silence, a
regiment in front would strike up one of the
patriotic songs, the next and the next would
take it up, until the volume of sound was lost in
the distance. It was thus that the good work
of all such men as Chidlaw was reinforced, and
the patriotic men of the old Union army stepped
up higher, and on to the broader platform, and
acknowledged the Fatherhood of God and the
brotherhood of man. Starting in only for the
patriotic purpose of saving the Union, and leaving the millions of bondsmen in their servitude,
they sang as they marched:—

> " As he died to make men holy,
> Let us die to make men free."

It was thus that the original 25 Abolitionists
of the 39th became 1000. The records show
that after the proclamation of Emancipation,
when the regiment was allowed to cast its vote
for State officers, all but five "voted as they
shot." Dr. Chidlaw's failing health, the second
year of the War, warned him that he was no
longer able to discharge the hard duties of the
campaign. When he retired, he took with him

the esteem and love of the entire command. It
is also true that he warmly reciprocated that
love; and all the years since, while he lived, he
kept in touch with the men of the old command.
I venture that there were few of the officers of
the regiment who personally knew, and came in
contact with more of the old soldiers of his regiment than did Dr. Chidlaw. If he was alive he
would object to being called "a great man,"
but it is only just to say, and to say with emphasis, he was an eminently just and good man.
His patriotism was interwoven with his religion;
and in 1861–62 but few orators stirred patriotic
men more certainly than did Chidlaw. One of
the happy traits of his character was, that he
never seemed to grow old in feeling. He loved
young people; and it kept his memory green
and tender and youthful, even when the scar
leaf of autumnal age was reached. The good
Quaker poet, Whittier, sang words of praise to
Thomas Shipley, which are fully applicable to
Dr. Chidlaw:

> " O loved of thousands! to thy grave
>   Sorrowing of heart thy brethren bore thee!
> The poor man and the rescued slave
>   Wept as the broken earth closed o'er thee;

And grateful tears like summer's rain,
    Quickened the dying grass again!
And there, as to some pilgrim shrine,
    Shall come the outcasts and the lowly,
Of gentle deeds and words of thine
    Breathing memories sweet and holy."

The beauty and incentives of such a life are, that the best things are made better, and the world of thought is lifted to a higher and purer atmosphere, and the human and the divine are united and blended.

(General Thomas T. Heath's tribute to Dr. Chidlaw, from a paper published in Loveland, O., August 24, 1892.)

In common with many of our citizens, especially our youth, the writer has pleasant memory pictures of "Brother Chidlaw," for he often ministered in our midst, as indeed he did "in all the churches," and in thousands of homes, far and near.

His presence was always and everywhere a benediction, and his life a benefaction. He loved everybody and everybody loved him.

In the camp of my command in 1863, he made a pulpit out of an army wagon, and melted veteran soldiers by his pathetic and eloquent appeals to men in arms for their country's existence, to enter also that higher service under the Captain of our Salvation, whose banner over us is love. I still have the little book, "The Christian Soldier," by Sir Henry Havelock, that he gave me one day, inscribed, "From your friend, B. W. Chidlaw."

The earth was full of work to be done. He never wasted one waking hour, would not remain tired, but rested himself with more work —work on both sides of the sea; in western settlements, and crowded cities; before Congress and Parliament; before the high and powerful; the low and the weak; to all alike he broke the bread of life.

On last Memorial Day, May, 1892, he came from New York to perform a sacred duty—to decorate the graves of our dead soldiers. Arrayed in his old uniform of Chaplain in the Union Army, he went with the writer and deposited roses on the graves of President William Henry Harrison, two revolutionary soldiers, and some forty-five comrades who fell in the war of the Rebellion, and were buried at North Bend and Berea. (This done, he invited the large concourse to the beautiful grove on his own farm near Berea, where the multitudes were fed.)

The speaker of the hour told the simple story of the Welsh boy in the picture, holding the U. S. flag—and—in imagination, the speaker and audience went to Radnor, Delaware County, and laid their choicest flowers on the graves of that boy's pioneer father and mother; then the speaker introduced them to the flag-boy, seated at his right hand, his friend—a sprightly youth of eighty years—Rev. Dr. Chidlaw!

There were tears and cheers and tears, when Dr. Chidlaw, with a clarion tone, called to the young people present to take a U. S. flag that one of the G. A. R. Post had set with its staff in the sod. When they had lifted it up, he said, " Wave it! Wave it! It is the most beautiful flag on earth. My father loved it, I love it, and when I die, I want it wrapped around my coffin. Oh! children, above all, love your country's flag, and love God!"

He bade us good-bye then, and the next day started for his birth-place, Bala, North Wales. He arrived there safely, in health and spirits. And on almost the very spot where he was born, on his 81st birthday, " he ceased his earthly work."

In less than forty days from the time when

he bade us a hearty "good-bye," his body, (brought back from Wales on Wednesday, Aug. 3, 1892,) rested for some hours in the same grove, where he had spoken so feelingly of the flag. According to his wish it was folded about him. After the impressive funeral services, Aug. 5th, his body was carried thence by loving hands, and laid reverently beside his kindred and soldier-comrades in Berea Cemetery.

Grand, Catholic, Christian, American man! Like thy Master. The common people heard thee gladly. Thou didst never speak or write a word which, dying, thou wast compelled to regret. * * * The poor, the fatherless, the widow in her affliction, were aided and comforted by thee. The example of thy good life—speaking with ten thousand tender and eloquent tongues, in sacred memories of tens of thousands, who knew and loved thee—shall live after thee, and proclaim to more boys and girls, and make plain to them, the power of the more than Archimedian levers by which thou didst aid to lift up the world. Faith, Hope, Love, these three— but the greatest of these is Love!

Farewell, old soldier of the Union and the Cross! I give thee the parting salute in sadness

Q

now. I will salute thee again in gladness, when the Archangel sounds the general assembly.

———

The Presbyterian Ministerial Association of Cincinnati, at a meeting held Aug. 1, 1892. unanimously adopted the following minutes:

The committee appointed by the Ministerial Association of Cincinnati, to prepare a suitable memorial of the life and death of Rev. B. W. Chidlaw, D. D., present the following:

The deceased, a member of this Association from its origin, was born in Bala, Wales, July 14, 1811, and died in his native place July 14, 1892, the day of the completion of 81 years of his pilgrimage. When about ten years old he came with his parents to the United States, and settled near Delaware, O.

His father died within the first year of his immigration, and his care and education were left to his mother, a most excellent and efficient Christian woman. He was a Christian from early life, and made a public profession in 1829, in connection with the Presbyterian church of Radnor, O. Even before this, he had consecrated himself to the ministry, and his struggle

for an education was marked by poverty, economy, sacrifice and perseverance seldom equaled.
His studies were persued privately, and in the
colleges at Gambier, Athens and Oxford, graduating in Miami University in 1833. He studied
theology under Dr. Bishop and the professors at
Oxford, and was licensed in April, 1835. For
several years before, he was practically a lay
preacher, showing himself apt to teach, and enjoying the favor of the churches.

Our dear brother spent a long life, eminent
for piety, zeal and usefulness. His labors,
which were incessant and toilsome, were given
to thousands of churches and committees, in the
pulpit and from house to house, in Sabbath-
schools and in prayer-meetings, and in poor-
houses and asylums, in hospitals, prisons and
reformatories, in schools, colleges and theological seminaries; nor should we overlook the great
work he did in the army under the Christian
Commission, on railroads and on steamers. We
know of no one who could more hopefully claim
the promise: " Blessed are ye that sow beside
all waters."

It should not be forgotten, moreover, that the
usefulness and appreciation of our lamented

brother were greatly increased and extended by his constant and successful use of the press, religious and secular, in keeping before the public the progress of religion, education and beneficence, and especially the wants and claim of penal and reformatory institutions.

In view of all these facts, this Association expresses its high appreciation of the ministerial character of our deceased brother, his great usefulness, his eloquence and fervor as a preacher, and his loving spirit manifested toward all.

The Association also expresses its sympathy with the widow and children, and prays that the God of all consolation may bless them in this sudden bereavement.

J. G. MONFORT,
W. H. MUSSEY,
J. H. WALTER.

CINCINNATI, July 24, 1892.

This Sabbath-school, as well as all Sabbath-schools of our country, have recently met with the loss of one of its dearest friends, Rev. Dr. B. W. Chidlaw, who died suddenly in Wales, on his eighty-first birthday. It is appropriate that some action be taken by this school, expressing its sorrow and sympathy, and it is therefore,

Resolved, That this school, in the death of Brother Chidlaw, has lost one of its dearest earthly friends, and that whilst sorrowing for the loss it has sustained, in common with all the Sabbath-schools of the land, and also in this its formal expression of sympathy, it has also cause for gratitude that God has so abundantly blessed his labors, and that he was spared so many years to engage in the work which enlisted his whole heart. May the Lord bless the work to which his life was devoted, and that the great Sabbath-school organization of our land may reap (whilst they are sowing) the benefits of his work. We bow in humble submission to our Heavenly Father's will and purposes in His dealing with His people, and pray that this dispensation of His providence may inspire the Sabbath-school workers to renewed activity in the work to which the life of our dear Father Chidlaw was consecrated.

Resolved, That we sympathize deeply with his family in their bereavement, and that a copy of these resolutions be sent to them.

Resolved, That these resolutions be spread on the minutes of our Sabbath-school.

> Central Congregational Church
> Sabbath School,
>
> HIRAM INGELS, Sec'y.

[Copy of action taken by the Board of Trustees of Miami University, at their annual meeting, held July, 1893, in regard to the death of Dr. Chidlaw, for so many years an honored and beloved member of the Board.]

MEMORIAL OF REV. B. W. CHIDLAW, D. D.

The committee appointed by the Board of Trustees of Miami University, to prepare a memorial notice of the late Dr. Benjamin W. Chidlaw, report as follows:

In common with all those who knew the late Rev. Benjamin W. Chidlaw, D. D., we express our high appreciation of his talents, character and usefulness. As a man, citizen and patriot, he performed his duties faithfully and well. As a Christian minister, as Chaplain in the army, as an educator, as orator and writer, and in all the departments of work in which he engaged, he did much for God, our country and humanity.

For his eminent services in all these respects we honor him.

But it is more especially of his services as a member of this Board that we would now express our high appreciation.

Receiving his first appointment as a Trustee of Miami University in 1863, he served in this capacity until his death, July 14, 1892, a period of about thirty years. During all this time, he performed his duties faithfully and efficiently. His judgment and advice were ever valued by his fellow-members. His long and valuable services as a Trustee, deserve the appreciation and gratitude not only of his fellow-members in the Board, but also of all the friends and patrons of Miami University.

Committee, {
   D. McDill,
   David R. Moore,
   D. W. McClung.

Miami University, June 14, 1893.

A TRIBUTE OF RESPECT FROM THE 39TH OHIO VOL-
UNTEER INFANTRY TO THEIR OLD CHAPLAIN.

While the 39th Ohio Infantry Volunteers (shortly after being mustered into service in

July, 1861), were camped at Camp Dennison, Ohio, preparing and getting ready for active service, attention was called to a man who was in the prime of life—never seeming to be idle, and who was continually visiting the hospitals of the camp, the barracks of the men, preaching sermons wherever an opportunity offered. That man was Rev. Benjamin W. Chidlaw. The Regiment having no Chaplain, the position was tendered him and accepted. The Regiment never regretted its action, and only regretted that God did not give him the health to remain with us longer. He was beloved by all men, and was not only the spiritual adviser of our regiment, but in his quiet, unostentatious way would perform the same service for any command.

He was destined, however, for a larger field of usefulness. After his resignation had been accepted, his fiery patriotism knew no rest, and we find him under the auspices of the Sanitary and Christian Commissions, visiting hospitals and battlefields, distributing supplies and administering to the wants of the wounded and sick, until after the days of Appomattox.

The following tribute of respect to his memory was passed at the regiment's second annual reunion held in Cincinnati, October 4, 1892:

" The cruel shaft of sorrow has since our last reunion penetrated our ranks, and our association has lost an honored, and one of its most useful and illustrious members. With profound sorrow for his loss, with affectionate remembrance of him as our Chaplain and friend, and with just pride in his Christian and manly character, this association formally records the death of Benjamin Williams Chidlaw, our late Chaplain—nay our late benefactor—on the date and place of his birth, on the 14th day of July last, in Bala, North Wales, aged 81 years.

" We remember, as if to-day, while in service, his firm decision of mind, his unceasing energy, his genial disposition, his everlasting good nature and his ever readiness to relieve our wants.

" A grand old man has departed this life, and the world was better from Dr. Chidlaw having lived. He has gone from this mundane sphere to glory. ' He fought the good fight, kept the

faith, finished the course, entered into his reward and received the crown.' "

> " Green be his memory,
> Mossy his grave."

Appendix.

SERMON,

PREACHED by the Rev. B. W. Chidlaw, Chaplan 39th Ohio Vol. Infantry, in the Amphitheater, Benton Barracks, Mo., on the occasion of the National Fast, appointed by President Lincoln, in September, 1861.

"If my people, which are called by my name, shall humble themselves, and pray and seek my face, and turn from their wicked ways, then will I hear from heaven, and will forgive their sins, and will heal their land." II Chron. VII, 14.

Never in the history of our nation have the people been greeted with a proclamation, inviting them to humiliation and prayer, under such momentous circumstances as those now surrounding us. Our national life is threatened, our Constitution and laws are assailed, and the horrors of civil war are upon us, and desolating our beloved country.

Our benignant Government, the best and the freest ever known, is imperilled by a widespread rebellion, and our glorious Union—for 85 years the hope of down trodden humanity—is in danger of disintegration. Anarchy and ruin stare us in the face. But, in our emergency, we are directed by our Chief Magistrate to look to a Rock that is higher than we, to trust in an arm omnipotent in power, and to call upon One who is mighty to deliver. Responding to this call of patriotism and religion, we are here assembled in the presence of Almighty God, acknowledging his supremacy over us as a nation, and looking to Him for guidance, strength and deliverance.

The record of our national history shows that God has recognized us as his people. Our origin was not in barbarism and pagan darkness. God sifted the nations of Europe for seed to plant in this new world. The genus was of his own planting. The Christian faith and morals taught by Divine revelation, the great principles of civil and religious liberty which obtained in the commonwealth of Israel, underlie the Declaration of our Independence; and the glorious Government founded upon its Christianity is recognized in our halls of legislation—in our courts of justice—in the millions of Bibles in the hands of our people—and the tens of thousands of Christian sanctuaries beautifying the cities, towns and hamlets, all over this broad land.

Our fathers acknowledged the government of Jehovah over men, trusted in it, and were delivered.

The sons of such noble sires have not ignored the faith of their fathers, nor swerved from their allegiance to the government of the Most High.

To-day the heart of every loyal citizen beats responsive to the call of our President, and, with this mighty host loyal to God and their country, around the altars of religion, we have gathered to humble ourselves under the mighty hand of God, that he may lift us up.

Our text reveals *the conditions of Divine deliverance in the day of our national calamity*—and to this subject I ask your attention:

This deliverance, which we so earnestly desire, must come from God; for vain is the help of man, for in the Lord Jehovah is everlasting strength.

To secure deliverance, we are summoned to the footstool of our God, to humble ourselves in the dust of genuine humiliation. Having, by our national sins, offended the Sovereign upon the throne, it is meet that we should bow with penitence subservient before Him, sincerely acknowledging our guilt, and with true sorrow seek reconciliation and forgiveness.

Our national prosperity has filled our hearts with pride, and we have forgotten Him who ruleth over all. Boasting of our greatness, glorying in our wide domain, from the prairies of the North to the everglades of Florida, from the Atlantic to the Pacific; proud of the unparalelled increase of our population, the wonderful development of our industrial energies, and our widespread commerce, as a people, this material prosperity has been our snare, and we have fallen into it. If to-day, as a nation, whose heart has been made gross by temporal prosperity, and who have forgotten God, we bow at His footstool, the divine faithfulness secures our deliverance from all our enemies. A nation, conscious of its national sins, humbled before God, and calling for the intervention of the Divine arm, will not seek in vain.

Second—Prayer; seeking the face of God is another condition of deliverance. There is power in prayer, and the duty of calling upon God in the hour of our peril, is pressed upon us from our relations to God, his promises, and the abounding grace of our Lord Jesus Christ. "Call upon me, and I will deliver thee," inspires our faith, brings us to the mercy seat, and makes us prevalent in our supplications.

Another condition of deliverance is named. God requires *the nation to turn away from its wicked ways.*

Our national sins are many and flagrant, and cannot be covered. The wrongs of the poor Indians; the clanking of the chains of enslaved millions; the prevalence of irreligion, profanity, intemperance, licentiousness, fraud and dishonesty; the neglect of the poor, and the idolatry of wealth; our disregard of truth, charity and righteousness, are the swift witnesses that stand up against us and condemn us.

To cover our national sin is not to prosper. Hiding a deadly cancer is not its cure. Moral gangrene at the national heart, unless removed, will stay its healthy pulsations, destroy its vitality. The Divine plan, alone, is curative. Turning from our wickedness is the sovereign balm, the only and sure remedy. Oh! if it could be applied to our individual and to our national heart—thus by the purging away of our sins by the blood of Christ, our moral health would be restored, our national life would be safe, and the God of the armies of Israel would fight our battles with us.

These are the conditions on which Divine deliverance is offered. Shall we accept them? The white flag of truce, the good will of God to the guilty, is sent unto us. Shall we accept to-day the proffered reconciliation? Shall we bow humbly before God, rend our hearts and not our garments, pray to Him, looking to the Lamb that was slain—the Lord of our righteousness, and our Redeemer? Shall we put away our wickedness, and transgress no more? *Then* God will hear. Yea, He will hear us from heaven, and save us by his mighty arm.

The deliverance promised if we accept and perform the conditions named:

1. *Our prayers shall be answered.* " *Then will I hear from heaven.*" There is power in prayer. It moves the hand of God. Hezekiah prays, and the army of Sennacherib is destroyed Prayer in Congress was as oil upon the water of strife, and hushed every rising tumult.

2. The Divine deliverance includes the *for-*

giveness of sin, and Divine favor. In the commonwealth of Israel, the sins of the people made the land to mourn. The heavens were as brass —pestilence, war and famine wasted the God-forgetting people. Prayer brought showers of rain, arrested the dark wing of wasting pestilence, and put the armies of the alien to flight.

3. The deliverance that the mercy of God secures is the restoration of peace—*" I will heal their land."*

The triumph of secession, the success of the rebellion instigated by it, is to inaugurate perpetual war, and to make the United States like distracted, bleeding Mexico.

To have peace, to heal our land, *the Union must be preserved, the supremacy of the General Government sustained, and its authority vindicated* on every inch of our territory. Loyalty to the Government is peace. To heal our bleeding country, rebellion *must* be suppressed. Disloyalty with uplifted hand cries out, " Let us alone!" and while the foundations of the Government are heaving, rebels and their apologists cry out, " Peace, peace, peace!" While this work of ruin, over which devils might hold a carnival, is progressing, woe to the arm that

R

would not smite the foe. God is to give us peace *through the triumphs of our arms* and the achievements of our navy.

Soldiers! you are sent of God to secure peace by crushing rebellion on the battle field. *Trust in Him; pray to Him; live for Him,* and our bleeding land shall be healed.

A THANKSGIVING SERMON.

Preached before the 39th O. V., at Camp Todd, Macon, Missouri, Nov. 28, 1861, by Rev. B. W. Chidlaw, Chaplain.

(Reported in the *Courier*, and prefaced by this editorial note: "We call attention to the able and eloquent Thanksgiving Sermon, by the Rev. B. W. Chidlaw, published on first page. Don't fail to read it.")

TEXT.—"O, give thanks unto the Lord, for he is good." Ps. cxvii, 1.

Every duty which God requires of his creatures is perfectly reasonable. As moral and accountable beings, we are the subjects of the Divine Government; our homage, and our obedience to God's authority and law, are righteous and reasonable demands. As dependent creatures, receiving every good and perfect gift, from His kind and bountiful hand, gratitude and thanksgiving should flow from every heart and burthen the utterances of every tongue. To-day, in nineteen of these United States, in accordance with a time-honored usage, the people, by the Governors of their respective States, have been invited to lay aside the cares and business of life, to think of the manifold blessings of Divine Providence, and at their homes and Christian sanctuaries, to offer fervent prayer and grateful acknowledgments to our Heavenly Father, for his abundant goodness and plenteous mercy.

We are assembled, this morning, under peculiar circumstances; far from our peaceful, homes, and in the midst of all the dreadful realities of civil war. Responding with glad hearts to the proclamation of our honored Governor, we have marched from our homes on the tented field, stacked our arms, and in this House of God, we would pay our vows unto the Lord, and adore with thanksgiving, His great and holy name.

Individually, we are the constant recipients of Divine favors, for in God we live, move, and have all the blessings which render existence such a blessing, such a boon.

The great expounder of the Constitution, nearing to life's last mile-stone, appreciating the blessings of life, exclaimed, " I still live!"   In the midst of death and its harbingers on the battle-fields, and in the hospital, we are, all of us here, alive, before God.   Life, health and reason are divine favors, inestimable in value, and indispensable for the enjoyment of life; these we have shared in rich profusion.

Our days and nights have been crowned with never-ceasing bestowments of Divine goodness. Our time has not been spent bed-ridden and sorely afflicted, our reason has not been dethroned, nor the raving of the maniac heard from our lips.   What a blessing is a sound mind in a healthy body!   Think of it, my hearers, appreciate its worth, and with humble, grateful hearts, give thanks unto the Lord your God.

Call to remembrance, also, the moral and spiritual blessing we have personally enjoyed. What power unseen, but real, has preserved you from the degrading dominion of those lusts and passions that war against the soul ?   Why has not habitual drunkenness dragged you down beneath its iron heel, brutalized your humanity, crushed your mental faculties, and hurried you down into a drunkard's dishonored grave? While others have fallen, you have maintained your ground against this monster foe. God helped you to stand; and to the integrity of your moral principles, and the fear of God, you owe this deliverance. Then thankfully acknowledge His goodness, and anew pledge fidelity at the altars of temperance.

*　　*　　*　　*　　*

The soldier, free from vicious habits, fortified with good principles, devoted to moral and intellectual improvement, holds in his own hand a God-giving passport to respect, usefulness and honor, wherever he goes. Napoleon, from his rank and file, gathered up Generals, Field Marshals and Kings. Your country will not fail to recognize and appreciate the moral, the intellectual, and the heroic claims of her gallant sons. Then, amid the trials and difficulties of camp life, Joseph-like, maintain your moral purity unstained, avoid the snares of guilty pleasures, turn away from the gambling table and the gilded saloon; devote, assiduously, your time and talents to military duty, moral and mental culture; then God will enrich you with all the treasures of His love, shield you with

His arm, guide you with his eye; and in the camp or on the battle-field, with you all will be well.

In our social and domestic blessings, we find abundant reasons for thanksgiving. Never before, on such a day, have we looked at our homes, and our loved ones there with such emotions of interest and gratitude. Here we are surrounded with homes desolated, society loosened in all its ties, upheaved with mutual distrusts and bitter animosities—the sad work of secesson. In our distant homes, beyond the Father of Waters, the prairies of Illinois, and the hills of Indiana, in the valleys of the Miami, Scioto, and the Muskingum, all is peace and harmony. No rebel hordes, in the madness of treason, pillage and destroy. As the shield of Divine Providence is over our homes, our families and friends, while our beloved commonwealth is blessed with peace and plenty in all its borders, let us joyously and gratefully give thanks to the Lord our God, and serve Him all our days.

In this day of our national peril, while armed treason is lifted up to destroy the life of a nation, to subvert law and order, to break up the tried foundations of civil government—to stay its cursed blows, to crush its malignant power, is a duty, an honor and a privilege, for which every loyal heart should give devout thanksgiving to the Ruler of nations. Did not the fathers of our nationality thank God for their high calling in behalf of human freedom, vindicated on every battle field of the Revolution ?

They, by sacrifices that we have read of, but never experienced, laid broad and deep the foundations of a free government, and eighty-five years of trial has proved it to be the best the world ever saw. The men of '76 laid the corner-stones of our free institutions, ordained of God, and the men of '93 reared the well-compacted and glorious edifice. The world has gazed upon it with astonishment and hope. In 1861, all civilized nations beheld with horror a bold attempt to destroy it—to raze its holy foundations, and build on its ruins a " Confederacy," founded on human slavery as its chief corner-stone. Is it duty to save your life from the assassin ? Is it a privilege to aid in arresting the lurid flames sweeping over your dwelling ! So, in the preservation of our Government, which God has founded and favored for

eighty-five years with his approving smiles, it is
our duty to pray that "God would arise and
scatter its enemies, and bring them down." and
to gird on the sword in His name, and as His
agents to crush the foe: and thus restore the
Union. maintain the supremacy of law, and
bring peace in all our borders. We should
thank God that He has given us a strong arm
and a willing heart to strike our manly blows in
this second war of independence. We are de-
fending the principles, the actions, and the
success of the men of '76. If truth and right
were on their side in the battlefields of the
Revolution, they are equally on our side in the
struggles of '61.

   *   *   *   *

To-day, with the great heart of loyalty in all
its pulsations beating in perfect harmony to put
down this wicked rebellion, so broad in its dimensions, and disastrous in its purposes, let us
give thanks to Almighty God that in this great
conflict we have not only the right on our side.
but might. Our resources to carry on this war
of self-preservation are abundant. In the loyal
States * * * we have near 20,000,-
ooo that have never bowed the knee to this

political Baal, which is worshiped by traitors and their sympathizers. These 20,000,000 believe in the divineness of human governments, and that the temple of our freedom is not to be undermined at pleasure, and a free people hopelessly crushed in its ruins. We have 3,800,000 fighting men, worthy of their sires, out of which the grand army of deliverance may be formed. Already, 500,000 men, brave and true, are in arms, and on the fields. A million more, in the spirit of the freedom-loving Bohemians, are ready to follow Ziska's drum whenever it beats.

Our own beloved, honored Ohio, has already sent out to the battlefields of right against wrong, 61,000 of her valiant sons. She has sent twenty-three gallant regiments to Virginia, to rescue the Old Dominion from the grasp of the destroyer. Eighteen regiments are in Kentucky, glorious old Kentucky, repelling the invasion of her soil; and in Missouri, two of her regiments have stood before the sweeping tides of rebellion and ruin. After this first fruit of loyalty to the Union and confidence in the government—this sacred suffering on the altar of patriotism—she has a reserve of 400,000 of her sons that she can send to the rescue. Ohio weeps over her gallant Lowe, and all her gallant troops that fell on the battlefields of Virginia, Kentucky and Missouri. Robbed of her worthy sons, that are cold in death or treated as felons in loathesome prisons, she will not withhold her treasures of men and money. All her energies, all her resources, will promptly respond to the call of our country in every time of need, and let our hearts redound with thanksgiving to the God of our fathers, that our great Commonwealth is so highly distinguished.

The amount of subsistence for the support of our vast armies is truly wonderful, and demands our grateful recognition and humble thanks. Our enemies look at their hoarded cotton; they can convert it to no available use; there is nothing to eat or wear in it. This King Cotton— their all in all—their strong deliverer—their bribe to the nations of Europe—is virtually in chains, helpless and hopeless. But what of the grain and provisions of the West, the commerce of the Atlantic coast, and the manufactories of the East ? Like mighty giants aroused, they are advancing to the contest. We can feed our five hundred thousand noble soldiers with abundance of the choicest food, and send an immense surplus to feed the famishing millions of France and England. And this supply of food is a bond that these nations shall keep the peace with the United States—a security against foreign interference—an assurance that we shall do our own work in our own way, none molesting or making us afraid.

The clothing needed by our army, we shall soon be able to supply. The wool crop of the United States, in 1857, was 18,000,000 pounds, and our hills are still covered with flocks, so that the 15,000,000 yards of cloth needed annually can be manufactured. Thus, in the providence of God, we can feed and clothe our vast army. The nation is not impoverished by this righteous war. The producing and consuming is among ourselves. * * * The nation is really strengthened in its material interests and vitality by this demonstration of strength in self-preservation. A national debt will be a light burden compared with the dismemberment of the Union, and the subversion of the Constitution. Money invested in the national loan will bind the people to a common interest in maintaining the integrity and perpetuity of the General Government.

In the prosecution of this war we have suffered some reverses. These have been mercies
in disguise, trials of our confidence in the just-
ness of our cause and the integrity of our purposes, for which we find reasons for thanksgiving. Our defeats have humbled our pride,
taught us lessons of wisdom, and really made
us stronger. They aroused and consolidated
our military power, as nothing but such mo-
mentary defeat could do. The barren victories
of our enemies at Bull's Run and Lexington
have not settled the question that the Union is
to be dissolved, and a new dynasty erected on
its crumbling ruins.

But they have gathered an army, with a young
leader, on the banks of the Potomac, whose ad-
vance will soon be felt at Richmond and Nashville. They have sent forth an Armada that has
leveled to the dust the strongholds of rebellion
in the very centre of its strength—the pledge that
ere long the starry banner shall wave on the
battlements of Moultrie and Sumter; and they
are now marshaling on the banks of the Mississippi a force which, blessed of our God, is destined to plant the old emblem of our nationality
over the Crescent City and the plains of Texas.

As a regiment, the Thirty-ninth O. V. Infantry has shared largely in the benefactions of Divine providence. The God of the armies of Israel has been our sun and shield. General good health has blessed our ranks. Only ten of our number have died. The maintenance of good order and sound discipline has elevated our regimental character, and given us a reputation worthy of reliable and gentlemanly soldiers. Let the *morale* of our regiment be sacredly maintained; yea, let our standard of moral and military excellence be elevated higher and higher, so that no honored parent, no loving wife or affectionate child, shall be sorrow-smitten or disgraced by our conduct, or our fate.

* * * True to each other, our country, and God, in trials and triumph, in joy and in sorrow, we shall aid our comrades in arms till victory shall rest on our banner, and our Government be vindicated and sustained—the Union indivisible now and for ever.

I add one other cause of our thanksgiving. While we see around us the blighting curse of secession, on once happy homes—on the altars of religion, the temples of learning, and the marts of trade—our loved Ohio is blessed with peace in all her borders. Her 2,360,000 of inhabitants have their sanctuaries opened for the worship of God. Over 12,000 school-houses echo the sweet hum of our children, quietly pursuing their education. Our fields have teemed with an abundant harvest; the din of industry is heard in our shops, and all departments of business give signs of activity and thrift. The majesty of law gives security to our homes; social life is not embittered by mutual feuds and rankling animosities. * * * * Peace and plenty bless our distant homes. No accursed rebellion has brought gaunt famine to stare them in the face. Starvation prices are not there; the necessaries and comforts of life abound, and none of our loved ones need suffer.

Enjoying the blessings of a benignant, just and free government, and now in the day of its peril, called to defend it from powerful and inveterate foes, let patriotism and religion nerve you for the conflict.

As a soldier, maintain the position and character of a true gentleman; exemplify the stern bravery of a gallant hero, combined with the virtues of true goodness. Always act under the authority of enlightened convictions of the good and true; cheerfully obey your superiors; study your duty, and do it with pleasure; honor the law in all its requirements. While you serve your government, let prompt, constant and cheerful obedience be your thank offering. In this warfare against lawlessness, stand up for the majesty of the law and its supremacy. In everything, be regulated by its authority; never let lawlessness stamp with its black stains the fair record of your soldier life.

Give to God the homage of your heart; believe and study His holy word; rest on His gracious promises; delight in His holy law, and lay hold on eternal life, the gift of God through our Lord Jesus Christ.

[From the Memorial pamphlet, published by special request, containing the funeral discourse delivered at Berea, Ohio, August 5, 1892, by the Rev. William Carson, A. M.)

" TRIUMPHA MORTE JAM VITA."

The pamphlet is thus prefaced by the publisher:

In the death of Father Chidlaw I have lost an old neighbor, a wise counselor and a valued friend, whom I have known and loved since early boyhood. I shall always cherish the memory of this godly man. This address, delivered at his funeral, is a full and complete analysis of his character, and well worthy of being preserved in permanent form. We have a beautiful illustration of the possibilities of youth, of the position of honor and influence that lies within the reach of any industrious and ambitious boy, however humble his early life may be. "Every man is the architect of his own fortune." Let our young men make the same wise choice, put the same vim and vigor into their work, and push right onward with the same dauntless courage, and they will find the world a paradise and heaven as their final good.

> " Lives of great men all remind us
> We can make our lives sublime,
> And departing, leave behind us
> Footprints on the sands of time."

WALTER HARTPENCE.

Dr. Chidlaw's body was laid to rest in the old family burying ground of Berea, near Cleves O. The funeral service was held on the green lawn, under the shadow of the big trees, within a stone's throw of the old homestead. The day was beautiful, and there was a great crowd. The venerable Dr. Monfort, senior editor of the

Herald and Presbyter, a classmate and lifelong friend, presided. A large number of ministers were present and took part in the service, among whom were Drs. Francis, Potter, James, Thompson, Jones, Griffith, and A. E. Chamberlain. It was an impressive hour, well befitting the close of this eminently successful career, consecrated to the service of God.

"Let me die the death of the righteous, and let my last end be like his."

[TRANSLATION of the Six Stanzas on " *Cwyn Pererin Oedranus,*" by the Rev. David Roberts, D. D., Wrexham,—a favorite hymn of Dr. Chidlaw's.]

AN AGED PILGRIM'S COMPLAINT.

I'm often like a pilgrim worn,
   Journeying alone,
Of all the friends I once possessed
   I hardly can find one.

So nigh you are, one step keeps me
   From you whom I love most;
Though near, you are too far for me
   To see you, shining host.

So nigh, the thickness is not more
   Than that of a fly's wing;
So far, that I can never hear
   A word you say or sing

So nigh, that in an instant I
   From here with you could be;
So far, immeasurably far,
   For you to come to me,

If no traversible path be found
   From that bright place to ours,
There is, through grace, a passage free
   From our place unto yours.

Along with Him, and in whose sight,
   Nothing is far or near,
I hope in heaven to join you all,
   Who are to me so dear.

            ALFRED, *alias* DEWI MEIRION.

www.ingramcontent.com/pod-product-compliance
Lightning Source LLC
Chambersburg PA
CBHW020946030726
47496CB00005B/1379